Minerva's Voyage

Lynne Kositsky

DUNDURN PRESS
TORONTO

Project Editor: Michael Carroll
Copy Editor: Cheryl Hawley
Design: Erin Mallory
Printer: Webcom

Library and Archives Canada Cataloguing in Publication
Kositsky, Lynne, 1947-
Minerva's voyage : a novel / Lynne Kositsky.

ISBN 978-1-55488-439-1

I. Title.

PS8571.O85M46 2009 jC813'.54 C2009-903259-7

1 2 3 4 5 13 12 11 10 09

Conseil des Arts du Canada
Canada Council for the Arts

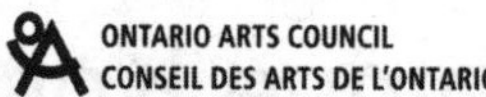

We acknowledge the support of the **Canada Council for the Arts** and the **Ontario Arts Council** for our publishing program. We also acknowledge the financial support of the **Government of Canada** through the **Book Publishing Industry Development Program** and **The Association for the Export of Canadian Books**, and the **Government of Ontario** through the **Ontario Book Publishers Tax Credit** program, and the **Ontario Media Development Corporation.**

Care has been taken to trace the ownership of copyright material used in this book. The author and the publisher welcome any information enabling them to rectify any references or credits in subsequent editions.

J. Kirk Howard, President

Printed and bound in Canada.
www.dundurn.com

Images from Henry Peacham's *Minerva Britanna*, used by permission of Special Collections at Middlebury College, courtesy of Professor Timothy Billings. Some have been digitally altered from their originals.

Dundurn Press
3 Church Street, Suite 500
Toronto, Ontario, Canada
M5E 1M2

Gazelle Book Services Limited
White Cross Mills
High Town, Lancaster, England
LA1 4XS

Dundurn Press
2250 Military Road
Tonawanda, NY
U.S.A. 14150

Mixed Sources
Product group from well-managed forests, controlled sources and recycled wood or fiber
www.fsc.org Cert no. SW-COC-002358
© 1996 Forest Stewardship Council

For Mich[illegible] my life partner;
Roger, my [illegible]riting partner;
and Tom, m[illegible]arring partner.

Chapter 1

From the Frying Pan to the Fire

I was stolen off the streets of Plymouth in the year of our Lord sixteen hundred and nine, by Master William Thatcher, better known as Scratcher, whose name and nickname I came to know in due course. It was the second of June, upon a Friday noontide, and the weather was waxing hot. The wind blew salt across the town. A multitude of holes in my hose allowed the damp breeze to reach through and cool my body. Scratcher had his sleeves rolled up above his elbows. We collided at the intersection of New Street and a small alley, where I was knocked on the head by Scratcher's wooden chest, which he carried on his shoulder and which travelled, at least in part, ahead of him. I fell down, stunned by the blow.

"Where do you live, boy?" Scratcher demanded. He dropped his chest and pulled me up by the ear.

"Nowhere, sir," I said. And this, for the moment at least, was true.

"Who are your parents?"

"None, sir." I felt a single tear drip down my cheek.

"Any who care?"

"No." This was true enough also. I sniffed.

He let go of my ear. "What is your name, boy?"

"Forgotten," I said. In fact, my name was Noah Vaile. I was more than glad to lose it because it sounded like "No Avail." Widow Oldham always made nasty cracks about it. If any of the other students asked me to do anything, she'd cackle and say: "Don't you see? It's hopeless. It is to Noah Vaile that you speak." It made me feel like a failure before I was even out of the starting gate. Returning to the present, I rubbed my forehead, which I was certain must be dented by the chest.

"Hmm. I will name you anew when the mood strikes me."

I threw him my best questioning look.

"I am in need of a servant: to fetch, to carry, to sharpen my quills." He was in need of a servant with no family connections; that was clear enough. "Pick up my chest."

"Well," said I, thinking as fast as I could while rubbing my head again.

"Stop that rubbing at once. Pick up my chest and be sharp about it."

I didn't like him. He was thin as a snake and looked horribly nasty, with two deep dark lines that ran from his eyes to his chin. And he kept scratching himself; he went at the scratching something furious. Besides, I was still weighing him and his intentions up. Who is easier to dispose of, after all, than a boy with no family? I could, in fact, see the tip of a knife hilt in his belt. It boded ill. But without him my prospects were dim, my next stop almost certainly the alms house. He had arrived, true it is, straight from Fortune, without turning left on the way.

My parents had vanished in a dense fog — the haze of the past, and also the very real smokiness of Plymouth town. Mistress Oldham, the schoolkeeper, had taken me in out of a confused blend of pity and laziness — she needed a slave — but had recently ejected me for setting rats free in the schoolhouse on Saturdays, and myself free during the week. I should have been studying and doing the housework, but was a certified truant who preferred pilfering to lessons and skivvying duties. The week she threw me out I pinched a chicken leg, a mound of apples, and a pigeon pie, all from St. Nick's market. There is a streak of wickedness in me, I'll willingly admit, but I've learned to live with myself as I am. There is no fixing wickedness: it arrives with a whoosh and a flash of its own accord. It makes no prior announcements. Sometimes my actions surprise even me.

"General truancy, is it? I can't abide general truancy even more than I can't abide rats," Oldham had screeched two weeks ago, pinching my ear just as Scratcher had just now. Adults seem to be overly fond of ear gripping, pulling, and pinching. In my case, it is their easiest hook to hang on to, the rest of me being too thin and slippery to grab a good handful of. Oldham knew nothing of my stealing, happily, or she'd have turned me over to the judge, and I'd now be hanged by the neck — boots dangling — until dead. I'd seen hangings enough in Plymouth, the convicted giving me a penny once or twice to pull hard on their legs after the drop and help their departure along.

I didn't want any young cozener pulling on *my* legs, thank you very much. I learned to run fast, really fast, so that I could outstrip the barrow boys whose stalls I nicked from. So if Oldham ever did find out my crimes, which, God knows, were hang-worthy, and decided to haul me to the judge, likely she wouldn't be able to catch me. In any case, her corns and carbuncles slowed her down. So did her enormous belly, which, when she so much as shifted from one foot to the other, quivered like a bowl of blancmange under her gown.

"Careful, boy. Stop daydreaming. There's treasure inside," Scratcher scolded now. I turned my attention back from Oldham's fat gizzard to his fat chest. His chest of the wooden, not the fleshly sort, I hasten to add. His fleshly chest looked more like a mine that had misfortunately suffered a cave-in.

"I haven't so much as touched the chest yet, sir." But my pulse twitched a couple of times. Spanish dollars were already glittering, big and round as silver plates, in my imagination. Treasure, was it? Scratcher could prove really valuable to me. My eyes must have lit up like candles on Sunday.

"Not that kind of treasure, you ignoramus. Intellectual gold. Poems and maps." His knotty face slanted sideways, and his loose neck skin creased into a wattle.

"Oh," said I, trying to ignore the fact that he looked like a demented cockerel and concentrate instead on his words. I'd spent two years in school trying to avoid poems and maps. But though I say so myself, I was sharp as a rapier, and much learning had rubbed off on me. What kind of poems and maps might these be? They were certainly not like those in the writing and cosmography lessons given by old dry-as-dead-bones Oldham. They would be treasure maps. With an X marking the spot. Ho ho. A shard of excitement flew up my arms, piercing my heart.

"Are you coming or not, sirrah? The hour is at hand." Scratcher managed to sound pompous and religious at the same time.

"What hour is that, sir?"

"You'll find out soon enough."

I chewed on the inside of my cheek loudly. I gestured into the northwest wind. But everything was performance, with him as spectator, because my mind was already made up. I had nowhere else to go, and there was also that treasureful mystery that had just cut deep into my heart and now tickled my brain. He cuffed me on the head. I jerked the chest skyward. He jumped back in momentary alarm, and I laughed in my mind. Then he nodded, turned, and veered along the cobblestone alley. I followed.

Chapter 2

Robin Starveling: A Playful Name

The hour was the hour of sailing. Unbeknown to me, I had been carrying a sea chest. If I'd have realized that the idiot was going to sea, I'd never have budged from my begging corner. I was terrified of the ocean. I was even scared witless of wells, would throw a rat hellwards to hear the dark splash. But I'd never look over the rim for fear of drowning. I'd seen others drown in the past, not in wells but with their ship almost to shore, their arms thrust above the waves, their voices thick yet shrill. Later there had been no voices, just the roar of the ocean and the nearby snarl of breakers. That was worse than the screams. Just like the silenced howls of hanged thieves and murderers, when they swung back and forth in the wind: The sound of no one. Yet here I was on a boat, the *Valentine*, as we rocked away from the dock. I'd tried to bolt at the last minute, treasure notwithstanding, almshouse notwithstanding. But Scratcher, as I came to know him, had tripped me up, shouldered his chest for once, and dragged me aboard by the hair, confirming with his treatment of me my already dubious impression of his nature.

Fearfully, I looked to the sea. We were in the company of other boats, their rigging tight as sinews, their sails slung out like women's petticoats. I counted six ships and two smaller pinnaces, all stuffed with souls. We were no different. Our own deck was as busy as the Bear Gardens at Candlemas.

"Bound for Virginia," an important-looking man shouted.

There was a ragged hoorah from the crowd, but a few travellers, men and women after my own heart, looked white as Monday's washing.

"Let me off. I don't want to go," I yelped.

"Don't worry. That's Sir George Winters, our admiral," said a dark-haired boy, pointing to the important-looking man. The boy was slightly smaller and probably younger than me. He wore an old black glove on his right hand, for reasons unknown, and sounded proud. "The admiral's a good seaman. He'll take care of us. But don't get on the wrong side of him."

"Thanks," I said. "I'll remember not to."

Winters didn't appear too frightening, not compared to some I'd come up against in the past, but I was terrified in a more general way anyhow. Virginia was the other side of the great ocean. The trip could take months. Maybe, despite what the dark-haired boy said, we'd fall off the edge of the world on the way. Or go down with our arms flung up, like the drowned sailors. I hadn't spent my time avoiding hanging so I could plummet to the bottom of the ocean.

"Virginia?" I asked Scratcher, still not really believing.

He didn't respond. He was busy scratching his arm, his face to the wind, his graying hair wisping out behind him.

"Chin up, Ginger Top," said a sailor, who was swabbing the deck. He smiled crookedly and rested his arm on one of several cannons. It was huge, snub-nosed, and black, and gave me not a whit of confidence. Were we to fight pirates, then? Or the vessels of the Spanish Main of which, even as a landlubber, I had heard too much?

"There's a name for you, sirrah. Master Ginger Top." Scratcher grinned, then spat through a hole in his teeth into the huge expanse of water beside us.

"Not likely, sir." Carrots was bad enough, and I'd heard that too many times to count.

He thought for a moment. "Starveling, then. Robin Starveling. You do look pared down to the bone, and that's a fact."

I frowned. Who was he to talk? He was skinny as a hungry rat. His hands had the scrawny look of hens' feet. But Starveling was as good a name as any, I supposed, though Heaven knows where he'd dragged it from.

"There was one called that in a play," Scratcher said, as if in answer to my thoughts, "when I was working in the theatre. He was just about as dim and as thin as you are."

Well then. Affronted I might be, but there was no way, after all, that I'd trust my real name, which was now buried in my brain, to Scratcher. He'd ridicule it for sure. Besides, the less he knew the better. Meanwhile, the more I found out about him the happier I'd be. Robin Starveling, eh? It had a ring to it.

I looked at the cannon again, fear rising in my throat.

"No need to be afeard, boy, of the sea. We s'll all make our fortunes."

"They say that the trees are high as mountains and the river by Jamestown wide as an ocean," whispered the dark-haired boy. He turned suddenly and clambered up the rigging. I kept my eyes down, too dizzy to look up. He disappeared from my view in a twinkling.

"Aye. An' the streets is paved with gold and the shores awash with diamonds and rubies. Ain't that so, Master Scratcher?" The sailor winked.

"Don't be stupid, Piggsley. There are no streets. And no jewelled sands. And the name, as you very well know, is Thatcher."

"Aye aye, sir." Piggsley tipped his threadbare cap.

Scratcher was now watching an ample-hipped woman in a red skirt as she swayed across the deck. When she disappeared below, he licked his thumb, dabbed mud off his hose, and slid slick as an eel through the hatch. "I must speak to her about the sumptuary laws," he said, halfway through. "Poor woman that she is, she has no right to be dressed in scarlet."

"That's Mary Finney," obliged Piggsley. "She does services for gentlemen."

"Does she indeed?" Scratcher grinned.

"Laundry services, I meant." But Scratcher was gone. Piggsley screwed his finger around his ear thoughtfully. "There's Will Scratcher, er, Thatcher, for you," he said. "We calls him Scratcher cause he's always scratching sundry parts of himself. Jes' now it was his belly. Other times he ain't so polite." Winking at me, Piggsley went on, "A single whiff of woman and he's away. Then he says it's his great sin. I seen him on other voyages."

So Scratcher had a weakness for women, did he? And Scratcher had also been on other voyages. I tucked these tidbits into the back of my brain in case I should have need of them. Then I upchucked my last meager meal of bread and wiped my mouth free of sick.

"Steady there, lad. We's barely out of port." Piggsley finished sweeping our part of the deck and moved on.

Sea travel didn't bode well for me. I felt better for being empty, though my mouth tasted bitter as aloe and the dizziness remained. And the blasted chest still needed to go down to the hold. No one would shift it except me, and I must have walked it damn near five miles this day, in and around Plymouth. I would best Scratcher for taking me to sea, I swore silently. And for making me carry his vile heavy chest crammed with maps and poems all around the town. It might take five days. It might take fifty. But I would best him.

Chapter 3

In the Belly of the Boat

We were sailing southerly and somewhat westerly. Or so Piggsley had told me. It was hot as hellfire below and stank of mold and filth and foot-rotted boots. The smell would surely choke us by the time July arrived, that's *if* we were still alive then.

"Hello again." The dark-haired boy I'd seen on deck was speaking to me. The heat didn't seem to inconvenience him. "Who are you?"

"Robin Starveling." I carefully parcelled out my words so as not to sound too friendly. Besides, though they too stank, I had boots and he had none. It placed me a notch up in the world.

"Peter Fence," he returned. "I'm the cabin boy."

As if I wanted to know. "I'm the servant of Master Will Thatcher." I threw my shoulders back to show my importance. Uncomfortable in that position, they soon slumped forward again.

"Scratcher's servant? You look right greenish and that's a fact. But redheads often do, even on land, and besides, you'll get your sea legs soon enough, never fear.

"I'm employed by Admiral Winters." He held his hand out, the one with the glove, and I shook it. But I kept my nose in the air as I did so, to one-up him a little and let him know I didn't usually shake hands with cabin boys — not even the cabin boy of an admiral. I was making a special exception for him.

"Pleased to make your acquaintance," I said. "Why do you wear that glove?"

He ignored the question. "I have to report to Admiral Winters." He saluted with his ungloved hand and raced up the ladder, two rungs at a time.

A few moments later, Scratcher lurched out of his hammock, buttoning his jerkin with one hand while scratching his private bits through his hose with the other. "Shake a leg," he told the heap of red that had been lying next to him. It was Mary.

A couple of sailors nudged each other and whispered something as she strolled away, picking up her stockings and shoes as she went. "I bin doin' his washing," she said. She winked.

"Stop smirking, Starveling."

"I'm not smirking, Master Thatcher. I'm imagining."

"Stop imagining, then. I don't pay you to imagine."

"Hell's Bells and little fishes. You don't pay me at all, sir." I felt this needed to be said.

Scratcher ignored me. His eyes were glassy as he stared after Mary, and no wonder. They'd been entertaining each other for hours. The hammock had jiggled most fearfully. I'd hoped it would collapse, but was unlucky. Maybe tomorrow, if he entertained her again.

"Stop rubbing yourself and get your bony backside off my coffer. I need to find something."

"Important, is it, Master Thatcher?"

"Important? Everything of mine is important. Can you read, you little weasel?"

"No, sir. Not the smallest squiggle. I haven't been taught," I lied. My tongue explored a painful hole in my tooth. Pain was an apt punishment for falsehoods. Or so that bitch Oldham always said when she whipped me.

"Your talk is amazingly genteel for an illiterate."

"Nevertheless, sir, I cannot read. Not even my own name. I expect that's why I forgot it. My mother was a gentlewoman, I believe, but she disappeared too soon to teach me."

"Ah. So you're an ever speaker but a never writer."

"I would be more than willing to learn sir."

"Never mind. You suit me better as you are." He threw open the chest. "Take hold of this." He slid me a sheet of paper with a picture of a three-masted ship on it. It looked like the *Valentine* in a storm, God save us. Underneath the ship was a poem. I struggled to read in the dimness, but the poem was written in a hand that was somewhat hard to make out. Scratcher snapped shut the chest and yanked the sheet from my fingers.

"Stop gawking, boy." He chanted the verse to himself then snorted, "Terrible rhyme."

"You could change it, Master Thatcher."

"Change it? Change it? I didn't write it, you ignorant buffoon. Master Plumsell did."

I was none the wiser, and said so politely.

"This is an emblem from Master Henricus Plumsell himself."

"What's an emblem, sir?

"Always a bloody question. I'll soon teach you to shut up." He thrust his face into mine. It was horrible, being so close, all warts and pimples.

I closed my eyes. "I'm anxious to learn sir, to do you better service."

Scratcher fell for my ruse. "Oh, very well. It's as you see: a picture with a verse or two under it, a diversion for the rich, who don't have much to do with themselves except play with emblems and complicos."

I wanted to ask him what a complico might be, but let it pass.

"The more you see and read an emblem," he went on, "the more it is supposed to tell you."

"How does it do that?"

"It just does. The verses and pictures reveal things."

"What sort of things?"

"Nothing a jolthead fool like you would understand."

I pressed on. "Where's it from?"

"Another apish question. If it's any of your business, I came by this one by, er, unconventional means."

He had pinched it, in other words.

"You nicked it, sir?" I just couldn't stop my mouth, which seemed to be forming words without benefit of brain.

"No. Nothing illegal, you absysmal apology for a cretin. I was visiting Master Plumsell to enquire after employment. He left it out on his desk with some other emblems. I'm sure he meant for me to see them. I didn't have the leisure to look them over while I was there, so I took them away with me." He coughed and scratched and seemed to gloat at what he'd done, as I might myself, had I done the same. But he also had a loose mouth, likely from drinking too much. This didn't bode well for me. He would ditch me when done with me, to keep his secrets intact. Or worse.

Stupidly, I pressed on. "Do you mean, Master Thatcher, that he didn't give you a job but you took your payment anyway?"

He cuffed me on the jaw, so that my own mouth got payment for being too loose. I cringed. "Sorry, sir. You did right, no doubt about it."

He stopped talking for a moment, as if deciding how to proceed. Should he trust me or shouldn't he? And did it matter anyway, as I was disposable? "Of course, I have every intention of returning them to him."

That was a lie, if ever I heard one, but I wouldn't let on that I knew. "Of course. I am on your side, Master Thatcher. No doubt about that either. I'm here to be your loyal servant and do your bidding." As I bowed, I was thrown off balance by a large wave and ended up sprawled on the floor.

"Look sharp if you wish to accompany me. Having a servant may increase my stature in Sir Thomas Boors' eyes, so I'll take you with me to him. If you behave. That's where I'm headed. We must carry the emblem to him right now."

"But we're at sea, sir," said I, wondering for a moment whether he meant us to walk on water. He was so full of himself I wouldn't put it past him.

"So is he. Don't you know a bloody thing?"

"Not much, Master Thatcher, I'm sorry to say. I am new to the shipping business, although I'm most willing to learn if you will teach me." I bowed again, this time without falling.

"Boors is in charge of the voyage," Scratcher said slowly and clearly, as if talking to an idiot. "He is in charge of the *Valentine*, and all the other ships in our fleet, although Sir George Winters is our admiral and better versed in sea matters. Sir Thomas Boors is blue blood, nobility, the servant of the King. He will be governor of Virginia — that's if we don't end up elsewhere. And don't blow your nose into your fingers in front of him, for the love of Heaven."

"Yes, sir."

He hit me around the head hard. It was a wonder I had any brains left at all.

"I mean no, sir."

But he was already gone. So I followed. And up above hatches we went.

Chapter 4

Emblem Enigma

Sir Thomas Boors was sitting in his cramped quarters at a desk strewn with papers and scrolls of various shapes and sizes. I could see maps and writing, more maps and more writing. He seemed oblivious to them. His small head, which protruded from his large ruff, seemed detached from the rest of his body as it bobbed up and down with every roll of the waves. His pointed beard made his face look as long and lean as a yardstick.

"Is there a fly in the room?" he asked, squinting at us through bloodshot eyes.

"That's just my boy Starveling, Sir Thomas." Scratcher shoved me into a corner.

"No, man. A fly. Of the insect variety. I thought I heard one buzzing."

Scratcher gazed around while scratching his threepenny bits, as I now called his private parts. "I don't see one, Sir Thomas."

"Ah, good. The little blighters are very dangerous to one's wellbeing, God knows." He blinked several times.

"Yes, sir." Scratcher fidgeted with the Plumsell emblem he was carrying. Although Boors didn't invite him to sit down, he eventually edged himself, crab-like, into a chair. I stayed where I was and tried to keep my balance.

"Especially if one swallows them. They tickle as they go down. And 'tis said they cause the plague." Boors' beard waggled when he talked. It was stained with old food and saliva, and he had a wild-eyed stare. Perchance he was mad.

I was beginning to feel rather queasy again, mostly at the thought that this man, blue-blooded and servant of the King though he might be, was likely also a total lunatic who was in charge of our well-being in the dangerous Virginia venture. Scratcher was a villain, but I'd choose evil over insanity any day. For one thing, I understood it better.

"Yes, sir," replied Scratcher. "It's very likely that they do, in my opinion." He bowed and scraped as well as he was able to while sitting.

"What? Did you want something, Thatcher … Scratcher … whatever your name is?" asked Boors, who had perchance forgotten that we were there.

"Thatcher, sir. It's very confidential, Sir Thomas. For your ears only." Scratcher leaned towards him.

"Aha." Boors looked interested at last. "Shouldn't you send your boy out then?"

"Don't worry. He's deaf as a post to important business. A real bumble brain to boot. Yet he certainly knows which side his bread is buttered on. Even though he's an illiterate lout. Isn't that so, Starveling?"

"Yes, Master Thatcher." I nodded vigorously though it made me feel more seasick. "I definitely know which side my bread is buttered on. It's buttered on your side."

Scratcher snorted. "Look at this, sir." He threw the emblem down on the desk.

I bent as far forward as I could, but Scratcher sat between me and the object of my attention. Meanwhile Boors mumbled over it as if casting a spell. There was a moment's pause. I needed a bath. My back was itching like it was covered in centipedes, but I didn't dare scratch it. Watching my new slave-master's scratching had mostly put me off the habit anyhow. I sat down on a pile of books and rubbed my back against the wall instead. At that moment Scratcher leaned back, and I could see. It was almost impossible to read the words on the emblem from my angle, but Boors was giving me time by tracing around the picture of the ship with a long crooked finger. I could just make out:

Go to the Isle of Devils, Truth doth urge.
We should avoid…

What should we avoid? There were more words above and beneath. The inscription was *Mente Videbor*. Latin, but I couldn't remember what it meant.

"Very interesting," Boors said suddenly, and Scratcher snatched the emblem picture with its accompanying verse off the table before I could figure out much more of anything.

"I agree, sir," said Scratcher. "I thought you ought to know. It was written by Master Plumsell, the well-known emblem maker and a dear friend of mine."

"Plumsell's a good man. Has he written about insects?"

"No, sir. Or at least, possibly bees. No flies so far. He was wrecked near the Isle of Devils some years ago."

The Isle of Devils? There it was again, just like in the verse. Where was it? What was it? One thing I knew for sure, it couldn't be Virginia. As the ship rolled, Scratcher grabbed the desk to steady himself, and the emblem flapped in his hand. Two words on the sheet leapt out at me. "Ignoble Cowardice." That's what we should avoid: ignoble cowardice. Whatever that meant.

"Ah yes, I remember," Boors said slowly. "All home safe in the end."

"All men home safe, most of them Frenchmen, but maybe not all *cargo* home safe. Plumsell is trying to tell us something," Scratcher said. My ears pricked up.

"Indubitably. I should inform Admiral Winters, though

damn me, the man hardly listens to me, arrogant nobody that he is. Bad family, you know. Atrocious manners."

"Don't take it to the admiral yet, sir, if you don't mind. We must figure it out for ourselves. It may be to our advantage. The emblem is mayhap from Plumsell's new manuscript, soon to be published, *Minerva Anglica.*" Scratcher tucked the paper into his jerkin. "It will show us the way. We must somehow get to the Isle of Devils."

"The Isle of Devils?" asked Boors, who seemed to have forgotten what they were talking about. "But we're going to Virginia."

"Yes, sir," Scratcher said patiently. "But we have to get to Devils' Isle before anyone else does. To claim the Golden Prize."

"The Golden Prize. Hmm. What would that be, man?"

"I'm not sure yet, sir, but it must be something richly extravagant. A treasure of some kind. Mayhap Spanish. Or Portuguese. In any case, I need a partner."

In crime, I thought, mentally rubbing my hands together.

"You, with your intelligence and wit, are the perfect person," Scratcher went on, inching towards Boors. "And it's the King's business." This was his second outright lie. Or at least, I thought it must be. But I needed to stop counting his untruths before I ran out of fingers.

"The King?" It was like a password. "Ah, yes, I see. Of course. God save his majesty!" Boors hoorahed, blinked, glared, and stood up.

Scratcher stood up too. The two men bent their heads together and spoke low. I couldn't hear four words in five, and the one I *could* make out was useless. "The other ships," I finally heard Scratcher say. The other ships *what*?

"You may go now, Starveling." Scratcher said, as if suddenly remembering I was there and at the same time measuring me for a coffin.

A beam creaked in the wind, and I jumped.

"Go line up for rations, boy."

"I'm not hungry, Master Scratcher." I shielded my head with my hands lest the creaking beam fall on me. And lest he hit me again.

"Why would I care whether you're hungry? I'm hungered enough to eat a piebald horse, so go line up, rumble fart. And fetch some ale. Take it down to the hold and await me there. The water is rank already. It stinks of horse piss. Get going."

Hell's Bells. That meant stumbling across the deck and queueing for at least half an hour in a crush of other would-be colonists, much bigger and stronger than me, all trying to push to the front. Where I couldn't miss the beery foam atop the waves, or the stench of cow meat, or my nauseating dizziness as I staggered around trying to keep my footing. I tried to delay. I clung to my corner. I blew my nose into my fingers and wiped my thumb and forefinger on my jerkin, contrary to instructions. But Scratcher again ordered me out. This time his hand furled into a fist.

He whispered again to Boors, though Boors didn't seem to be listening, busy as he was swatting his imaginary fly. Where and what was the Isle of Devils? And what was the Golden Prize? And why had Scratcher chosen Boors, of all people, to be his co-conspirator?

"Now we've rid ourselves of him, Sir Thomas, let's get down to some real business," I heard Scratcher say as I shut the door of Boors' cabin. Whatever the business was, and whatever Scratcher thought, I decided I would be, at the very least, a partner in it.

Chapter 5

New Alliance

Back in the hold my wickedness was reasserting itself. In fact, it had an absolute passion to open the chest to find out more about the "business," and was using me as its instrument. But although I was the most willing servant in the world, the chest stayed most obstinately shut. I tried it, pried it, banged it, kicked it, but nothing helped. I knew there had to be a secret button or clasp on it somewhere, and started to search for it, running my fingers swiftly across its top and sides. But after a minute or two I noticed Mary Fish-Finney hanging around and stopped abruptly, shoving my hands behind my back and adopting an innocent air.

"What you doing?" Mary asked sharply.

"Nothing, mistress."

"Where's your master?"

"What's it to you?"

"None of your business, toad spawn." People always seemed to be saying that to me. "Where is he?"

"If he wanted you to know," I retorted saucily, "he'd tell you himself."

"How dare you? Don't you know who I am?" Her face had flushed bright red to match her skirt.

"No, mistress, and I don't much care. I serve my master, not you. He wouldn't thank me for telling strangers of his whereabouts."

She was livid. "I ain't a stranger. I know him."

That was right enough, at least in the Biblical sense, but my stupid mouth was quicker than a fighting cock out of the cage to say so.

She snarled. I snarled back, longer and larger. But even my fingers pulling down my lower lids with my thumbs stuck up my nostrils couldn't get rid of her. She circled, picking her way over and over again among voyagers, blankets, bundles, and all the other rubbish that littered the hold. After a bit she snorted and climbed into Scratcher's hammock, her holey shoes sticking out the top. When she fell asleep, I went back to my investigations, keeping a sharp eye out for Scratcher.

Just as I was about to give up, I felt something give under my fingers. It was a knob of some kind, hidden inside the lip of the cover. I lifted the top until there was a crack between it and the bottom, then doubled over and squinted.

Papers were inside, quite a few of them. With inky writing and drawings. I opened the chest a fraction wider, dying to see more. At that moment, as fate would have it, Scratcher started down the ladder. In a trice I slammed the chest shut and sat on it.

"Where's my meat and drink?"

"Here, sir." They were on the floor beside me.

He grunted and was scoffing a mouthful when the holey shoes caught his eye. "What are you doing in the hammock, Mary?" he cried, spitting food in all directions. "This meat's tough as leather. Did I not tell you to go away?"

"My dear..." came a sleepy voice, "I thought you'd be in need of a bit of cheering up."

"Well, I'm not. Get lost. I'll tell you when — if — I want you."

Mary climbed out and shook herself. "You want to watch that boy of yours, Scratcher. He ain't honest. He was in your bloody chest." She took herself off. Two children and a chicken squawked out of her path.

Scratcher thrust his chicken-bone fist under my chin and lifted it.

"It's not so, sir. She's trying to make strife between you and me, true it is," I whimpered. "In fact, your chest was hanging a little open when I got down here, and I made sure to close it for you. Perchance it was her who had opened it. I wouldn't know how."

"It's either you or she, sirrah. One of you is lying. One of you isn't worth a gob of spit."

"It's her, sir. She's lying to pay me back. She wanted to know where you were, and I wouldn't say, loyal to my master as I was. I know where my bread is buttered, as you've said many a time."

Scratcher punched me hard in the belly. "That's for if it was you. And this will be too." He took out his knife and waved its sharp point in my face. "Stop snivelling. If it was her, she'll be the one to see my ire. I'm not one for hitting women, but I'll do it if I'm pushed. And I'll keep my eye on both of you from now on, you truculent trickle of snot. See if I don't."

Peter Fence was suddenly at my elbow. "I saw the whole thing, master. A woman was delving in your coffers. This boy here had nothing to do with it. He tried to close the lid on her. He almost succeeded in shutting it on her fingers."

"Why didn't you say, so, Starveling?"

I thought fast. "Because you wouldn't have believed me, sir, honest to a fault though I am."

Fence had saved my skin. Scratcher swore, opened the chest, checked it quickly, and snapped it shut, before taking an enormous bite of the leathery meat and washing it down with ale. He spat out a lump of gristle.

The emblem was still in his jerkin. It had to be. He wouldn't have left it with Boors. I'd get to it sooner or later, when he was drunk or fell into a deep snore of a sleep.

Fence had surprised me. He had acted like an ally. I wasn't used to that. I was suspicious of everyone I met. Mistress Oldham had beaten me, and the other scholars had pummelled or spat at me, mostly because I was poor, only minorly because I was wicked. But I realized, upon reflection, that Fence's actions had seemed loyal and true from the beginning. Of course, "had seemed" is not exactly the same thing as "were."

"What was it you were looking for in the box?" Fence asked later, while I, back turned, was pissing in a pail.

"A picture. Perchance a map. You lied for me."

"I never lied before, and wish not to make a habit of it, but I'll play lookout for you if you wish."

"The next time I go on the scavenge?"

"Aye — if you want me to. Then in return you'll tell me why the thing is so important to you."

"A bargain! Do you read, Peter Fence?" asked I, having straightened my hose and rubbed my sore belly, which was still feeling the force of Scratcher's punch.

"No, Robin, not more than a few words. But I can count right well. It was my job to count the sheep out to pasture. Then I had to count them when they came back to see if any were missing. So I know my addition and my subtraction. But all this counting was before my daddy died and I came to sea."

Aha. Counting, although a valuable skill to keep in one's pouch, was my downfall. It wasn't taught in school, and I had never developed the knack of it. I would run out of numbers the moment I ran out of fingers. Fence could definitely prove useful, I decided. I had obtained my own partner in crime, though I still wasn't sure that I entirely trusted him. After all, hadn't I told Scratcher I couldn't read when I could? Mayhap Fence had done the same kind of lying with me, though true it is he said he'd never lied before. But that could be a lie also; however, I could tell Fence as much or as little as I chose to, and thus make him into my servant, just as Scratcher thought he had made me into his.

We still had weeks or even months at sea. I could take my time about sniffing out Scratcher's "business." That way I'd be more likely to succeed. And I'd find the treasure before Scratcher did or die in the attempt. My beating him to the trove would pay him back for his filthy treatment of me. As to what I would do with the treasure when I got it, that was another matter entirely, one that I couldn't figure out till I knew what it was.

Chapter 6

Damn that Fly!

Days passed and I was careful to be careful. I didn't gainsay Scratcher. I didn't question him. And I had no opportunity to open the chest or hunt through his clothes, which he wore to bed, like most of the passengers. So I didn't get myself into further trouble. Instead, I managed to keep my wickedness at bay while gaining, or mayhap regaining, Scratcher's trust. I plied him with whatever food and drink was available, though he was the most disgusting eater I'd ever seen, taking huge mouthfuls, gagging, and spitting biscuit mixed with saliva and weevils far and wide. Otherwise, I tried to act as if I wasn't there, and so he seemed more at ease that I was. In fact, he took me with him when he next visited Boors. It was steaming. We could have fried eggs on the cabin floor had we possessed any. And the boat was heaving up and down with each huge wave, heaving my insides up and down too. The sickness kept growing in me. But Scratcher and Boors hardly noticed. They were too busy.

"In the event that the ships are separated in a simple storm or hurricano," dictated Boors, with much prompting from Scratcher, "All captains are to sail their craft to the Baruadas in the West Indies. We shall meet up there." Scratcher was writing the words down, his eyes almost crossed.

"Why did you tell me to tell them to go there?" asked Boors, the supposed author of the note.

"Because although we'll soon be south of Virginia, no one in his right mind would sail to the Isle of Devils, even if told to. The seas are high, the rocks are terribly dangerous, and it's full of shipwrecks, mostly Spanish, which have foundered there. We'll send the other ships elsewhere. We don't want them. We'll try for the Isle of Devils alone."

"Why would we do that?"

"The Golden Prize, Sir Thomas, the Golden Prize. Remember?"

"Oh, er, yes." Boors clearly didn't.

I listened intently while sharpening the quills. That was my job. Scratcher's plan didn't sound very sensible to me.

"Now copy that out five more times, Rat Catcher," ordered Boors, who was still under the mistaken impression that he was in charge.

"The name is Thatcher, Sir Thomas. Not Rat Catcher. And I would appreciate it if you would remember that. This should work like a charm." Scratcher dipped his quill. "Whoever heard of crossing the great sea without encountering at least one tempest? In fact, it's getting rough already."

Indeed. The ship pitched. I staggered across the cabin. Ink splattered on the floor. Blue blood, I thought.

"You, you tripe-visaged rascal, come back here," admonished my master. "Mop up that spill. Then roll up each note that I write and stick it with wax."

I did as he commanded. "So Baruada is actually not the Isle of Devils?" I asked. I already knew the answer to this. It was merely my opening gambit in what I hoped would be a long game of verbal chess.

"No, boy, it's the Isle of Goats," said Boors. He bleated twice, much to my astonishment. "You see..."

"Don't grace that saucy fellow with further information, Sir Thomas, if you have any. Best to leave his head as empty when he goes out as it was when he came in."

"Ah, yes, of course." Boors bent the ring on his finger to the warm wax to impress his seal on it. "Sorry, boy." He bleated again. And truth be told, he did rather resemble a goat, with his long bony face and sparse beard.

"We should now give your notes to Proule, Sir Thomas," said Scratcher, "and order him to take the small boat and row out to give them to the captains of the other ships. That way, Admiral Winters won't be involved." Sweat cascaded down his skinny cheeks.

"Proule?"

"One of the mariners. Bald. Beer-stained moustache. Broken teeth."

"Right. Of course. Send Proule in," said Sir Thomas.

Scratcher slipped out and returned with him in less than half a minute. Proule must have been waiting right outside the door. This didn't particularly surprise me. It did seem to surprise Boors, however.

"What are you doing here, Proule?" he asked.

"You sent for me, sir."

"Ah, yes, so I did. Why was that?" Boors blinked twice, unhappily.

"Dunno, sir." Proule looked confused.

"The notes, Sir Thomas," hinted Scratcher in a loud whisper.

Now I realized. He chose Boors to confide in because Boors' power was useful, but five minutes later he wouldn't remember a single word that Scratcher had said. Who could keep a secret safer than that?

"Yes, yes, the notes. Take the notes, Proule."

"Aye, aye, sir," said Proule. Unknown to Boors, he and Scratcher often stood in corners of the hold and muttered to each other, meanwhile throwing meaningful glances at Scratcher's tightly closed chest.

While Boors was simply being used, Proule was doubtless Scratcher's real partner. He smelled of something nasty.

Cat pee and stinking sweat, with other putrid smells hovering around his person but unidentifiable. Not that a soul on board smelled clean, we all had a rottenness about us lately, but his stench was especially loathsome. It erupted from his pores and became even more disgusting when he opened his mouth, whether to speak or sneeze. His breath could slay dragons, his teeth were mere stumps. They looked like black gravestones.

His friendship with Scratcher, which was peppered with insult on both sides, drove Mary to distraction. She'd been banished from the hammock permanently, but still wanted Scratcher to herself for reasons I could easily imagine. She didn't want interference from Proule or anyone else. But Scratcher had said to her, as he sent her off, "Get away from me or you'll be sorry. You are my great sin." He tossed her what looked to be a penny or two. She blamed anyone she could think of for her loss of him and his apparently new found religious fervour. But her hatred for me — she now pinched me hard whenever she could get hold of me — was only a puny shadow of her hatred for Proule. When he came within her sights she bared her teeth and flared her nostrils like a beserk horse. Proule, not to be outdone, thumped her arm or backside — whatever was available — to force her to shift.

"Look up there, boy," Boors continued now, staring at the ceiling. "No, not there. There. For heaven's sake, swat that blasted fly for me."

"Yes, sir." I waved my arms violently in the air. "I got it," I cried, clutching an invisible bluebottle.

Scratcher, meanwhile, was instructing Proule on what he wanted done with the notes. Boors thanked me and I grinned. Though it was now clear as glass that Scratcher was the boss in this enterprise, I needed to be in the good books of both of them. And Proule too, if I didn't want to find myself in the bottom of the sea with pearls for eyes. He was scary. Mary mattered less than the shit pail in the hold. When we reached land I would be done with her. Or so I thought.

Chapter 7

Scratcher's Ambitions

Two days later, the wind was blowing strong but friendly, pushing us along quite handily. The storm hadn't materialized. I had heard Piggsley say we would reach Virginia within the fortnight, and so no longer feared every moment that we would soon all be drowned dead. But I still felt greenish, as Fence would have put it.

"You s'll soon get your sea legs, lad," Piggsley assured me, every time he saw me.

I was waiting for them to be delivered.

Scratcher was ignoring me today. He was scratching his leg and his threepenny bits. I'd faded into the woodwork, in a manner of speaking, into the timbers of the ship, too familiar or contemptible to be taken into account. At least, he and Proule were talking as if I wasn't there, and that was fine with me. I still had to bend forward to hear them, though. The racket below hatches was appalling. It seemed to grow louder with each passing day. People arguing, children skriking, and beasts, those that weren't yet eaten, lowing or squawking for all they were worth. The din, together with the heat, was even getting to Proule and Scratcher.

"We sail too far south, man," complained Proule. "We'll never get where we're going this way."

"Not so," replied Scratcher, looking dangerous. He stopped scratching and stroked his knife hilt.

"The other ships is burning up with fever. I couldn't get away fast enough when I delivered them letters from Boors. I was afeard for my life and health." Proule was sitting on a hogshead of ale and picking at what remained of his teeth with a large splinter.

"There's no helping it." Scratcher countered.

"The wind blew fair for a while, but now we're tacking in the wrong direction."

"We have to go south, you dithering numbskull, or we'll be blown all the way back to England. But it is to our advantage. Let the simpletons on the other ships think we'll come up the coast to Virginia after we've crossed."

"Don't yer call me a numbskull." Proule wiped the splinter on his jerkin, leaving a long smear.

"No, Proule, my fine handsome fellow, you're quite right. I forgot myself. I'm too used to speaking to that jelly-livered drudge over there." He pointed in my direction. "But all we need is a spot of rain and lightning and we'll look like we're making for the Baruadas, as stipulated on those letters you delivered. In truth we'll make for the Isle of Devils."

Proule hiccupped.

"I know what I'm doing. I've been much employed, had jobs in high places," confided Scratcher, who had been drinking gallons more ale since our water had gone stale, and was talking too freely, as usual.

"And yer've been thrown out of most of 'em, as I've heard." Proule, too, had been tippling, but unlike me, he hadn't learned when to hold his yap.

Scratcher bent down and thrust his face into Proule's, eyes popping. "Who told you that?" A few men turned to stare at him before going on with their business, such as it was.

"I dunno."

"Piggsley, I'll be bound, with his loose lips." Scratcher toyed with his knife again.

"No, Master Thatcher. 'Tweren't him." Proule drew back. "Sorry, sir. I got beyond myself. It's the drink in me talking."

"Watch your mouth in future or I'll watch it for you."

"Aye, sir, Master Thatcher."

Scratcher pushed him off the hogshead and sat on it himself. "I'm the most important person in this dungeon of a hold. Boors wants me for secretary in Virginia — or wherever." He waved his skinny hand in the air.

"That's good news," muttered Proule, staggering up and trying to look agreeable, a rather difficult task given his features. His face finally rearranged itself into a horrid grimace beneath his bald pate, his tombstone teeth on display. I couldn't blame him for trying though. Eventually everyone knuckled under to Scratcher. He could be fierce and frightening as a corcodillo, and corcodillos ate men and boys whole, didn't they? Or so Oldham had warned me when I wouldn't recite my Latin.

"I play along," said Scratcher. "But I mean to make my fortune. Don't want to work for any man but myself anymore."

"And so say all of us, every man jack of us. Amen." Proule sat down on the dirty floor and took a long draught of ale. Scratcher drank also, his legs splayed so wide he almost fell backwards off the hogshead. They both hiccupped. It was time for me to find out more. While they were both so drunk they'd sleep like the dead. With Fence as my lookout, I would go scavenging this night. I crossed myself for luck.

Chapter 8

Horrible Proule the Ghoul

Midnight at least. Hot as an oven. Quiet, except for Scratcher's snores, which shook our part of the hold. Fence lit a stub of a candle he'd brought from Boor's cabin. His face haloed in the dark. I put my hands on the chest, felt around for the secret knob, and pressed. The lid sprang open.

"Move the candle over here," I hissed. "I can't see."

Fence sniffed, scrunching up his nose, and lifted the candle. The circle of dim light moved from his face to the contents of the chest, and I started to rummage through them. An emblem. Another emblem, neither of them the ship in the storm, which Scratcher must still have about him. And finally, a third emblem.

"Look at that!" I whistled.

"Shh. What is it?" whispered Fence. "I've never seen anything like it before."

"It's a cipher wheel. Right there on that emblem. It's

used to decipher secret messages. And it's telling us there's a hidden message *here* that we have to decipher. I'm sure of it."

"Take it out."

"No. I'm only going to look, and maybe take one small thing so Scratcher doesn't notice. If we take a wad of papers, he'll smoke us out right away. Besides…"

"There's only so much you can hide under a holey shirt and threadbare jerkin," said Fence.

"True it is."

Fence was not such a dunce, after all.

I went back to the chest and riffled under the three emblems. All that was beneath them was a mysterious piece of vellum. I stared at it. The alphabet was on the left in separate columns, with a different arrangement of x's and y's by each letter.

"What's that?" asked Fence, sniffing again.

"I'm not sure. But it's important as hell or my name's not Robin Starveling," said I, examining it. "Hold the candle closer."

A xxxxx G xxyyx N xyyxx T yxxyx
B xxxxy H xxyyy O xyyxy U/V yxxyy
C xxxyx I/J xyxxx P xyyyx W yxyxx
D xxxyy K xyxxy Q xyyyy X yxyxy
E xxyxx L xyxyx R yxxxx Y yxyxx
F xxyxy M xyxyy S yxxxy Z yxyyy

It wasn't very clear despite the light cast by the candle, but I kept looking at the vellum till the x's squiggled up and down and began to jig. What could it all mean?

Scratcher's snores ceased, and he moaned. He was waking up! My heart clip-clopped. I inched the chest shut, but still kept ahold of the vellum. Fence pinched the wick of his candle. After a sickening silence that seemed to last till doomsday, Scratcher's breath caught and he began to snore again.

"This way," I whispered. We crawled on hands and knees over bundles and boots, until we reached the ladder beneath the hatch. It was still slung open to draw in fresh salty air, such air, that is, as would consent to brave the fug and travel down to the colonists.

My purpose was to climb up to the deck, sick though it would make me to see a seascape unanchored to land. I would be able to view the vellum more clearly up there. But before I shinned the ladder, a cloud above passed, and the man in the moon peered in upon us, making it light enough to see. I started to examine the x's and y's again, Fence getting in the way more often than not. For a small boy, he certainly had an incredibly big head, and he kept thrusting it in front of mine to get a better look at the sheet of dancing and mysterious letters.

"Move your bonce," I said, annoyed.

Just then, fingers grasped my shoulder hard, nails digging into my skin like grappling hooks. "Get off," I yelled.

My cries disturbed the dreams of one or two travellers, whose pale faces stared at me for a moment, before their owners blinked and fell back to sleep.

A growl. The sickening stench of farts and tomcats and sour wine, stronger than all the other stinks of the hold. As the nails dug even deeper into my shoulder, I imagined blood spurting from crescent-shaped wounds.

"Give over. You're killing me."

"Shut yer yap, cockroach."

I turned, though I already knew who it was: Proule, that coffin-mouthed ruffian. My belly heaved.

Chapter 9

It's a Cipher!

At that moment the *Valentine*'s prow churned out of the water, hurling me into him. He shoved me backwards, punched me, and before I could recover, tore the vellum from my hand.

"What the ruddy hell is this?" He flapped the vellum. The moon shone in. His bald head reflected it.

I could taste blood. My belly heaved again. What could it be that wouldn't incriminate us? That wouldn't send Proule howling to Scratcher? I couldn't think of a damn thing.

"I said, cockroach, what the hell is this?"

Fence had slipped as the ship nosed out of the sea. He came crawling slowly on all fours, his head down.

"Please, Master Proule…"

"What?"

"It's a list of my duties from the admiral, Sir George Winters, good Master Proule." He began, baby-like, to suck the tip of his thumb.

At this point I noticed Proule was holding the vellum upside down. Could he even read? I decided to chance it. Taking my cue from quick thinker Fence, I said, "All those things on the left, they're the days of the week, enough for a month. Next to them are the duties. Sweep the deck; take Sir Thomas Boors his dinner; empty the piss pail and shit buckets overboard." I had seen Fence perform such-like duties before.

"Why would the likes of yer be reading it in the middle of the ruddy night?"

"He forgot a duty, sir, yesterday, the dinner one, and got in trouble with Sir Thomas Boors." I felt sure that if asked, Boors wouldn't remember one way or the other. "We were figuring out where Fence went wrong — he's not much of a reader, and I'm a worse one, sir, true it is. Why, some days I can barely read at all."

"Aye, sir." Fence's head came up, and his thumb came out, his expression earnest. "We were figuring it out so I wouldn't make the same mistake again and come in for a good thrashing."

Proule looked from Fence to me and back again. Then he squinted at the page, one eye shut, turning it sideways and over and right side up. No question about it. He didn't trust us, but he couldn't read. The rogue was flummoxed.

Fence stood up. "It's mine! As I told you, it's from the admiral. And if you don't give it back, I'll tell him you've stole it from me."

"Yer shan't if yer know what's good for yer."

"I'll do it, sir. I will." God be praised. That boy had real guts.

Proule flinched, then thrust his head forward. He opened his mangy mouth wide as a corcodillo basking in the sun. For a moment I was afraid he was going to snap his rotting fangs shut on Fence's nose. But, "Yers, is it, yer cheeky dog? Don't yer be wasting my time again, y'hear me? I'm an important man with important doings."

He ground the vellum into his palm, screwed it up, then tossed it away. As he ran up the ladder, taking his rancid reek with him, I crept over to retrieve the crumpled sheet. I smoothed it and stuck it in my shirt, relief flooding my veins. I had a sudden thought and took it out again, holding it beneath the open hatch. The moon illuminated the script for a moment, disappearing as the ship lurched and we tacked southwest into the dark night. But I'd had enough time to check my theory. I'd been right. What I had here was a cipher key. A real one, sure enough. Though as to what it was supposed to *de*-cipher, and how I or anyone else was supposed to decipher it, I had not a single clue.

"Tomorrow," I mouthed to Fence, tucking the cipher away. "Tomorrow we will talk."

He nodded, and lay down right on the spot to sleep, one arm curled around a rung of the ladder, the hand of the other holding his candle stub. He looked amazingly peaceful, considering all that had happened.

For the first time in my miserable joke of a life I knew that I had a true and gallant friend. It was a strange feeling, not entirely comfortable, like the prickly sensation I once got from an old woolen jerkin when I had no shirt to wear under it. But the jerkin, though itchy, had been warm. And the thought of having a real ally was both itchy and warmish too.

I found a place in the wooden skeleton of the ship, two curved ribs with a narrow gap between them, in which to stow the cipher key. The next night, when the hold was dark and as quiet as it could be with its gaggle of voyagers, littler voyagers, and beasts, Fence and I took it out and examined it until the candle he was holding melted down and scorched his fingers. But I was a quick study and by then I knew the pattern of it off by heart. We still didn't have the meaning, though, which it refused, quite obstinately, to yield to us.

"There is a meaning to it, though, I'm sure," I whispered to Fence at noontide, knocking as many maggots as I could off a bloated piece of salt meat with an iron nail I'd found. Some of them held on tight, but I couldn't bear to actually touch them.

"Right you are."

"Each letter is represented by five x's or y's, or a mix of them. It must stand for something."

"If we could get some of the other papers in the chest, it's likely they'd give us clues," said Fence, who had scarfed down his foul meat and biscuit, worms and weevils and all.

"I've learned the cipher key down to the last x and y. It's burnt on my brain."

"Good on you," Fence grinned at me. A last shred of beef was visible on his tooth.

"But we should return the damn thing. We're lucky Scratcher hasn't noticed it's missing, but he will, true it is, if we hold on to it much longer."

I shut my eyes tight, shoved the meat into my mouth, and swallowed it quick, barely chewing. I had to eat. My rags were so hanging off me that I had tied my long hose on with string purloined from one of the crew. But my gorge rose at the thought and certainty of the worms, which had gone down my gullet hanging onto the meat like sailors clinging to a barrel after a shipwreck. I felt a feathery movement in my throat. My mouth filled with grease, vomit, and drowning maggots.

I pushed by Fence, by chickens and voyagers and lumpy fardels, and sped up the ladder to the deck, spewing the meager contents of my belly over the side.

"Sorry you're sick. But cheer up. It's raining. That should cool us down," Fence announced as he joined me.

Raining it was. After days and days of burning weather. Still hot as Hades, despite what Fence said, but raining. Mist obscured the hot eye of the sun and the other ships as the warm and welcome drops fell on my upturned face. The relief, however, didn't last long as the sea was beginning to roil. During the night, feeling sickish for a second time as the sea grew rougher, I stole a last look at the cipher by candlelight, making sure I knew every x and y of it. The small guttering flame went out as we hit a large wave. I tucked the cipher under my shirt to return it to the chest, but could not for the moment, as there was too much hurly-burly in the hold. The sea quietened some at last, and the voyagers quieted also. Too tired to move, I drifted to sleep where I was, every so often waking as damp entered through crevices in the deck above, cramping my knees.

"I couldn't return the bloody thing," I told Fence the next day. I was rubbing my calves and trying to stretch my legs back out to normal. The wind was rising again. "I'll put it back between the timbers."

"Between the timbers?"

"Isn't that what I said?"

Fence could have his annoying moments too.

"No, Robin, don't do that. Keep everything important to you right close about. A huge storm is coming. I feel it here." He pressed the front of his head. There was a pinched look to him, as if the devil had caught his nose and twisted it around and around.

"Keep everything important to you right close about," mocked Mary. I hadn't realized she was standing behind us. "Keep everything important to you close about, young cowards, lest we sink." She tweaked my ear. "Ha ha ha. Skin and bones toad like you will drown in the blink of an eye if the ship goes down."

"Fat fish like you will sink to the bottom of the sea and drown first." But I shuddered.

"Fishes don't drown." Mary stalked away.

"No more do toads," I yelled after her, trying to be brave.

Chapter 10

Pelted by Mary and Rain

The rain continued. The ship reared up to the roof of heaven and down to the depths of hell.

"Don't worry, this be'ant dangerous," Piggsley said, as he went upstairs to the deck. "I'm to my bed. I'll take the dog with me so he don't go overboor." This was the ship's dog, who had of late been following me around like I was a meat bone. Even hard shoving didn't deter him. He could stand his ground without so much as a baring of teeth.

I loved animals for the most part but I hated dogs, filthy, wormy creatures. They'd taken a bite out of my rear end often enough in Plymouth, and they were notorious for pinching food from barrows that could have gone into my own belly. Ma Oldham had two hugely fat, bad-tempered lapdogs whose names were Trusty and Ruffles, or Rusty and Truffles, I could never remember which. Neither of them was averse to taking a nip out of my ankle, too short they were to reach my bum. So I was glad to see this one disappear, at least for the moment, especially as he did his business wherever he happened to be. And I kept stepping in it.

I was still thinking about tempests, about dogs and their villainous ways and their confusion of names, when something sharp sped through the air and hit me on the head. It bounced away before I could see what it was. I thought at first it had come out of the hammock, which swung alarmingly. My forehead must be bleeding. I clapped my hand to it. I felt a sticky wetness and a hard pain. I staggered up with a loud cry. It was Mary, and the witch was laughing. Her hand reared above her shoulder, her fingers still splayed open. She'd cut me. A small cut, but a cut nevertheless. Soon, if I wasn't careful, I'd be as brainless as Boors.

"A stone. I meant it for your better," she cackled. "Scratcher, I mean. Pig that he is. Shame it missed him. Lucky it hit you." Incredible! She was more interested in revenge than safety, even with us jouncing up and down in the hold as if on wayward horses.

She cackled again. "I've been through this before. I'll go through it again in the future. This ain't nothing to what I've seen. I ain't afraid of a rogue wave or two."

Scratcher had been sleeping most of the day and evening, between bouts of drinking. He snorted and woke now, gripping the sides of his hammock. His knuckles were stretched taut. He took one hand off the canvas and fumbled in his clothing. After a moment he pissed in a huge arc onto the floor. He was worse than the bloody dog. His eyes were glaring, first at Mary, then at me. His face was grey and menacing in the half dark.

"She cut me, Master Thatcher, with a stone."

"Shut up or I'll cut you worse." The two deep lines running down his cheeks looked in the dimness as if they'd been painted on. He lay back down.

The ship rolled. He suddenly sat bolt upright. "I must go see Boors immediately." He sounded stone cold sober, and was struggling to put on his jerkin as his hammock rocked precariously. "I must get to his cabin. Starveling, you bone bag, my boots have slid away. Find my goddamn boots." Boots on, with no little help from me, he rushed up to the first deck. I went after him.

"Stay below," he commanded. "Who told you to follow me, carrytale that you are?"

"Carrytale, sir? Not I, on my life. Merely your servant, here to aid you in all your endeavours." We were under the top deck. Heedless sailors lay in hammocks, covered by the deck above. But it still rained in at the sides, and the sea was high and ominous. I tried to assure myself of our safety. After all, the mariners seemed unperturbed by the storm; they had doubtless been through rougher waters in the past. But true it is that one careless move, one slight push, could pitch me or anyone else into the water.

Scratcher moved among the crew and across the deck. I took his silence as assent and followed close upon him. He was already knocking on one of the doors of the middle rooms. No response. He banged harder. Boors appeared, in nightgown and cap.

"What is it? Is there a fly? I thought I had them quite cleared out despite the hot weather."

"No Sir Thomas. It is merely I, William Thatcher, come to remind you to keep your promise."

"Promise, promise. What promise is that?" He took off his nightcap and scratched his head in bewilderment.

"In the event of a storm, Sir Thomas … you remember, surely?"

"Of course I remember." He paused. "What is it I remember, exactly?"

"Make for the Isle of Devils."

"Of course, of course." He neighed.

"Tell Sir George Winters to do so," prompted Scratcher.

"Sir George…?" Boors was, if anything, getting worse.

"Winters. The admiral."

"Oh, yes, of course. I'll tell Sir George Winters right away, sure as shipshape."

"That's if there can be any making for anywhere in this weather," muttered Scratcher, water running down the deep lines in his face as if they were trenches. "And that's if Winters will obey your commands."

"Yes. Thank you. Good night," said Boors, ever the gentleman. He put his cap back on.

"Good night, sir," I replied.

"Old fool," Scratcher said, as Boors closed the door on his own thumb and was obliged to open it again. He let out a yelp, and his straggly beard bristled.

A wall of water poured over the deck. The cannons groaned, straining against the ropes that held them in place. We scrambled for safety as the pilot was thrown off balance and fell from on high among us; he seemed unhurt, racing back to the helm to try to direct the ship. Boors, who had been following us, scurried back to his room.

That afternoon there was a lull, but later the wind grew stronger, roaring without cease, so loud that we could hear it below, despite the usual din. Rain pelted the hatch, a small stream of water leaking through it and down the ladder. Water was coming in also through gaps in the timbers. Those who had fallen asleep began to wake and moan as they tried to light lanterns. I had been cowering in a corner, legs drawn up, but now rose and pushed my body against the tilt of the boat so I could reach a wooden support and hold on.

The ship creaked as though about to split in half. Children were howling. Women and men were shouting and trying to hang onto their belongings, to one another, and to the upright supports, as I did. A memory of meat and maggots came back to me, and I threw up into the bilge.

"Look to my chest, you snivelling fish brain," yelled Scratcher. The chest, like much else in the hold, was sliding across the wet floor. A barrel was sliding too, before falling on its side and rolling.

"Look to my chest, I said. And stop that keg, before it bursts and the hold is awash in beer."

I meant not to budge, whatever Scratcher said, but lost my grip and fell over when the ship's prow reared up and out of the water. I slid like an eel along the floor as the boat lurched violently down. There was nothing for me to grab hold of. I had lost my place and the supports were few and far between, already thickly surrounded by others fighting to keep their balance; everything seemed in motion. We listed to the right. My feet hit the side and for an instant I was anchored. Then, as the boat listed the other way, I began to slide back. My shoulder hit the chest and I stumbled up and sat on it. It moved little after that, but I felt that at any second I would be hurled elsewhere. The beer barrel hit it too, coming to a sharp halt as it did so. Then it rolled again, exploding beer into the water. Everything else slithered and skidded as the ship reeled.

"Dear God, I want a dry death, any death but this. Dear God, save me from the sea," I implored over and over. "I swear I will never listen to the whoosh and flash of wickedness again." I clung to the chest. But the wind and rain only grew more violent.

Fence hurtled down the ladder, tripping over a rung in his haste.

"We were sleeping on deck," he said, "until the tempest grew right wild. Then I was sent high into the rigging to help furl the sails. Another sailor up there toppled into the ocean."

"There was no rescuing him?"

"We passed him in a second as the ship was driven on."

"Not Piggsley?" My heart skipped. "It wasn't Piggsley?"

"I saw little. The gale lashed my face, blinding me." He was drenched and trembling.

"Perchance, with a bit of luck, it was Proule." As the words left my mouth, I felt shamed. I hugged Fence. "Hell's Bells and Cockle Shells, thanks be that you're safe."

"Thanks be," he echoed, his blue eyes dark and wild.

He and I clung to each other, true it is, through the dark hours, though I could barely see him. We were violently shaken and sick. In spite of the heat, my teeth chattered, sure that we were on our way to hell or already there. God and all his angels were elsewhere, if they were anywhere at all. There was no creature, neither earthly nor magical, to ease us through the hideous commotion of the tempest. Would we even live till morning? I didn't think so.

Chapter 11

No Hope!

Finally day arrived, though it hardly grew lighter. I pinched myself to make sure I wasn't dreaming. It hurt, so I decided I wasn't.

The cipher, soaked though it might be, was still under my shirt. But what good could it possibly do me? The wind dropped a little, but water was streaming through the timbers and rising in the hold. I could feel it around my ankles and splashing onto my knees. And then, quite suddenly, it was at my thighs. Cold, cold water. I gasped. The hatch opened and the sea and rain poured in from above too. Jagged lightning lit the hold. Two sailors rushed down the ladder. I'd seen them many times before and named them after Oldham's lapdogs, Trusty and Ruffles, because they looked like twins and were always together, and because I didn't know their real names. One of them at least looked trusty. The other was walleyed.

"The caulking is forced out from the ribs," cried Trusty.

"The timber never set," shouted Ruffles, managing to look every which way except at the rising water. "The ship was too new."

"Damn the Company," cried another mariner, who had just come to join them. They set to work mending the leaks with anything they could lay their hands on. The passengers sometimes helped, other times yelled or fought with the crew as their clothing or linens were seized and squeezed into the spaces between the wooden ribs.

One sailor found pieces of salted beef in a fardel to stuff in the holes and sop up the liquid.

"What shall we do without food?" screamed a woman.

"How will you eat when you're dead?" asked the man I knew by now to be the boatswain, descending with a candle to find more leaks in the ribs. Others followed. Candles, although protected by hands, blew out faster than their owners found seepings. Meanwhile the sea continued to pour through an undiscovered hole, and the rain, huge swathes of it, blew in through the open hatch till someone slammed it shut. Now the weather below had changed. Now the hold was cold as ice. Both Fence and I were up, helping to stem the leaks. I fought a man for his loose kerchief, and shoved it into a hole. He pushed hard against my belly and I stumbled and fell into the whirling liquid, swallowing a mouthful of its foul ingredients before scrambling up again, brine pouring through my nostrils. The water was still rising.

"Man the pumps," cried the boatswain. "Fetch the buckets. Every man to work, crew and passengers all. Ladies, hold back there. Look to your children."

And indeed almost every man did set to work. So, to my surprise, did Mary, her long hair dripping like seaweed, her red skirt floating around her, as she tried with a pail to rid the hold of water. Her skirt would buoy her up, I thought, if we were all cast into the sea, though she would look like a huge scarlet jellyfish. I got a turn at the pump, and pumped till my arms were numb and like to break. She took over from me without a word. She wasn't laughing now. Afterwards I filled buckets and ran up the ladder with them, emptying them into the sea, until we set up a long line of boys and men who passed the full buckets up from one to another, emptied them, and passed them back down. For the most part, shirts had come off in the wet, though I kept mine and my jerkin about me. They were all I had, and besides, the cipher key was still safe beneath. I would need it now, if we ever reached land. I had, in my fear, forgotten everything about it I had ever learned.

We pumped and emptied buckets for hours. But it seemed hopeless as the water rose and rose. Then, in the middle of the day, when it seemed the storm could not worsen, blackness descended completely, and I could hardly see my own hand directly before my eyes. We were lost and forsaken by God in endless storm, endless cold, and everlasting night.

It came to me that there was no way out. A single lantern still cast a dim circle of light in the hold, but many had stopped bailing, though the pumps were still in operation. We would all drown in this huge and empty sea.

The sky continued black all that day. We were besieged on all sides. Water still poured from the heavens and was yet discharging into the hold. I took another turn at the pump, though my arms were failing. Then the pumps failed too.

"They are clotted with bread," yelled a sailor. "Bread from the bake room."

The blackness above afeard us all. People were crying. Men were praying loudly. Women were shrieking as they held their children out of the rising waters. Some had already climbed to the deck, but it was probably as dangerous there as anywhere, as the huge waves could knock them into the ocean. Suddenly Admiral Winters was before us, barely visible but shouting over the wind and tumult. The ship's minister accompanied him.

"Calm yourselves," cried the admiral.

There was little response.

"Calm yourselves, I said."

His voice was so commanding that soon all voices were quieted, and in their place there was only the howling of wind and the driving force of water. Although the admiral was thought by many to be a good man, his face, a sinister pattern of shadows in the dark hold, belied that belief. But at least he didn't seem mad, like Boors. He had the rock-hard voice of sanity.

"We will ride out the storm, I do believe and trust to God," now spake the minister. "But we must all pray." He got down on his knees in the water and began to give thanks, although for what, I was not entirely sure. A few voyagers, mostly the loud prayers of the last few hours, joined in.

"Where do we make for?" shouted a woman with a small child in her arms.

"We travel southwest if 'tis possible. We make for wherever the storm drives us and will hope for land," the admiral replied. There was a long groan from his audience. Had Boors spoken to him? It was impossible to tell.

"But I come to tell you that to save ourselves we are obliged to lighten the ship so it rides higher in the water."

A mariner nodded, but the colonists, surrounded by all their earthly goods, some of which were now floating, grabbed hold of whatever they could, cradling as much as possible in their arms with their babies and children.

"Take your possessions on deck. They must be jettisoned."

"No," yelled Scratcher, emerging from a dim corner. "I shall not." He was the only man who had not made any effort to help bail the ship. But now he was the first man forward.

"A possession, whatever it is, cannot be worth a life. Carry your possessions to the deck. This is a direct order."

"No," shouted Scratcher. "I shall not yield my chest. It is full of important documents." He hauled it up, dripping as it was, and hugged it to him.

"We have to unburden the ship. Your sea chest is going overboard. The papers inside are likely already destroyed by brine. If you do not wish to be separated from it, that is, of course, your decision and your right; you will be thrown overboard with it."

"I am on the King's business," screamed the enraged Scratcher.

"The King is not in charge here. I am. And I have no time for displays such as this. You will not get your way no matter how loud you scream." Sir George Winters sneered faintly before turning away from Scratcher. He motioned to his crew.

They moved in, grabbing possessions from others and the chest from Scratcher. He made a last desperate effort to fling the top open and retrieve his papers, but it was slammed on his hand by a burly mariner. He cried out.

The minister prayed ever more forcefully, and began to sing a hymn.

"You, boy," shouted Winters, "take this box up on deck."

I complied, more afeard of Winters than of the tempest and Scratcher combined. My feet slipped on the rungs, and the chest was a great burden as my arms were so stiff and cold, but I managed to get to the deck, pushed aloft by those behind me, all scrambling to quit the hold.

Scratcher's chest was taken from me, heaved up by a crewman, and tossed overboard. There was finally a dim light emerging from a break in the clouds, so I could watch the chest as it reared and circled with other boxes and bundles on the roaring spume once, twice, three times, before sinking, its precious secrets lost. I yawled at the loss of it. Barrels of beer went into the water too, and many other fine casks of drink and foodstuffs went under. I didn't care. I felt so sick I was sure I'd never want to eat again. There was much wailing and cursing, but apart from that one yawl as the chest went down, I was silent, defeated, half-blinded by rain. Meanwhile I held on to the ship's icy rail very tightly, not wishing to disappear into the ocean myself. Even now I didn't want to be swallowed up a moment before I had to be.

"Then I looked on all the works that my hands had wrought, and on the labor that I had labored to do: and behold, all was vanity and vexation of the spirit, and there was no profit under the sun," cried the minister, who had climbed on deck himself and was watching, almost smugly, or so it seemed to me, as the sea swallowed our goods.

"Cheerful fellow you are," a man called out to him.

The admiral had been right, though he told his version of the truth differently from the minister. Life was worth a good deal more than chattels, even treasureful ones. All my wicked efforts to retrieve Scratcher's emblems now seemed stupid. And I could also see that they had been useless. Fence and I were left with a cipher key but nothing, it would seem, to *de*-cipher. Fence, thank goodness for Fence. As if he'd heard my thoughts, he popped up next to me, grabbing my arm and looking mournfully over the side. Despite everything, courage began to return to me because he was there. And praise be, next to Fence stood Piggsley, who I'd feared drowned. At first I thought he was grinning, but his face was set in a hard and salt-drenched scowl.

The minister was yelling above the gale again. "Let us then hear the conclusion of the whole matter: Fear God, and keep His commandments, for this is the whole duty of man."

"Oh, go blow your nose," the same man called out, clearly willing to risk eternal damnation.

"Hell's Bells, we're in terrible trouble, aren't we?" I asked Piggsley. I wanted him to contradict me.

"I s'll tell you, Ginger Top. We's not looking good. We's not looking good at all."

Scratcher had not followed me up though the hold was filling rapidly. No doubt he didn't wish to risk being sent for an even bigger swim. But my courage, which had spiked for a moment, had already begun to wane. I believed we should all be drowned soon. And that would be the real end of the matter.

Chapter 12

Over the Rail

We were everyone of us on deck now, despite the danger, hanging onto spars, to rails, to rigging, and to one another. The hold, in spite of our best efforts to bail, was full of bilge, a dusty fog rising from it. Even worse, the ship was listing very badly, to *starboard*, as Fence would have it. For some reason I'd always thought starboard meant the left side. It sounded left-sided to me, as if the meaning were in the word itself, but Fence had put me *right*, so to speak. I had been so wrong about so many things, both big and little. I had thought life a bad but funny jest, but it wasn't a jest at all. It was deadly serious. It was all I had of value. And true it is, soon our ship's *right side* would be beneath the level of the ocean, and we should all slide across the deck and tumble to the bottom of the sea.

The bottom of the sea. The words haunted me. I could only think over and over of the drowning men I'd seen off

Plymouth shore, their arms thrust up, their voices thick with fear. But numb with cold and shock, I was quickly losing my own fear. I was so tired I began to wish only that our disaster be played out, as theirs had been, and for us to be lying thoughtless and careless on the ocean floor. I worried no longer about the Isle of Devils. We could never reach it, or any other island, even if Boors had so instructed Admiral Winters. And even if Winters had *listened* to him, which was most doubtful. Nobody, just about, really listened to Boors.

Scratcher stood by a railing, his face grey in the dimness. He clipped me round the ear hole as I went by, just for good measure. He had given up shouting about his precious chest but was mayhap still searching for it in the rolling waves. In the end he took the emblem of the three-masted ship from under his jerkin and pitched it into the ocean, where in a trice it became waterlogged and disappeared.

"What are you doing?" I shouted, but it was too late.

"Useless it is now," he mumbled.

"Cut the ropes of the starboard cannon to free them," shouted the boatswain, whose own face was as pale as that of a hanged man. "It's our only hope. Throw all them ordnance into the sea." Out came knives of every sort. Ropes were severed, and half the cannons, our only protection, were heaved overboard. They sank immediately, the ship straightening somewhat before beginning to list slightly to larboard.

"S'll we free the larboard cannon too?" shouted a seaman.

"No, sirrah. Release the mainmast from the shrouds, and cut her down by the box to relieve the pressure, or we'll still be done for."

"And you boys, get rid of the bluebottles that are sent to plague us, for the love of God," said Boors, who had come from his room to see what was going on. He was still wearing his night cap. "I can't hear myself think for the roaring of the flies and the shifting of the furniture."

"Aye aye, Sir Thomas," responded Peter Fence. No one else took any notice except Admiral Winters, who was standing close by watching the men follow orders.

"Get to your cabin," he hissed through his teeth at Boors.

"But the flies are Devil sent. Punishing. Whizzing like whirligigs all over the place."

"Get to your cabin, I said."

"I am in charge here. I am Sir Thomas Boors. You cannot tell me what to do."

"I can and I will. I am in charge at sea. You are creating a disturbance. Do as you're told."

Boors stuttered as if about to protest, but then peered into Winters' face. It was set and stern. "Very well," said the knight, staggering off into the wind like a drunken man. "But mark my words, I shall be in charge on land."

"If the ship ever gets there, we will decide," Winters called after him.

No one else appeared to be watching them. The men, sailors and colonists both, were too taken up with managing themselves and the ship in the tempest, and that might be for the best. Our situation was terrifying enough. Who needed to know that except for Winters, if he could prevail, our fate was in the hands of a complete madman?

The crew were busy unknotting the shrouds, while we cleared a path for them by crushing ourselves into a yet smaller area. A great cry went up from the exhausted passengers as the mainmast toppled like a huge tree in a night forest. It hit the rail, slid by the board, and vanished instantly, together with its sail yards, as the hurricano shrieked and whistled around us. The ship almost overturned as the mast went down into the deep, and as it tipped back with a great creak, waves rose over the side and flooded the deck. We went reeling. Boors, further down the deck, was yelling again about the furniture. Voyagers, struggling back up, were promising to light candles, to go on pilgrimages, to enter monasteries, if only they might be saved. As wind and voices rose in a crescendo, a rat skittered by me and leapt into the sea. He was, I thought, sager than any of us.

CHAPTER 13

THE VISITATION OF ST. ELMO

Quite suddenly, there appeared on the foremast, which was still in place, a trail of small glowing lights, yellow and white, dancing along the cross made by the mast and its yards, following their leader. They flew from shroud to shroud, streaming past Winters, who had mounted to the poop deck and was on the watch.

"St. Elmo," Fence said with awe. "I never thought to have seen it."

"What does it mean? What can it mean?" I clamoured, as a sigh went up from bone-tired passengers and crew.

"It means we be'ant like to die, Ginger Top," said Piggsley, who was standing near. "Look up, boys. There is more lights aloft. St. Elmo, St. Helen and St Nicholas. Castor and Pollux as they's named by we mariners in the old times. Heaven be praised."

"Aye, Praise be. Like bright candles in the night," said

Fence, in wonderment. "Like little balls of fire."

But my own wonder was mixed with disbelief. Could I be dreaming? Or even drowned dead in a shipwreck but imagining still? The phantoms of St. Elmo and St. Helen, as I now thought them, divided and burned on the rigging and around the rails, before vanishing into the cabins, through the hatch and into the hold, as well as across the deck and over the side of our vessel. I watched them flaming on the sea for a short while. Soon they extinguished, leaving faint round lights in their wake.

The wind was already dropping and the darkness clearing. The rain reduced to a drizzle and what was left of the ship, its skeleton really, now sat low and quiet in the water. The weather was beginning to warm slightly. It was a miracle, and many threw themselves on their knees to give thanks. But the sea was empty. Of the rest of our fleet there was not a sign.

Fence guessed my thoughts. "Perhaps they have gone on to Virginia."

"Or perhaps they are drowned," I responded sadly, having been so close to death myself.

Then came the words we thought we'd never hear.

"Land ahoy," cried the admiral from his high perch. "Land ahoy."

And indeed, as I looked, I could see a huge shadow on the sea, a presence before us, like a crouching beast in the water. I was not at all sure that this was really happening. But if this was the dream of a drowning boy, I fervently prayed never to wake from it.

Chapter 14

Goodly Land

Fence and I had found a piece of wood and floated to land on it, too excited to wait for others. And now we were on what Oldham would have called *terra firma*. It was amazing the ship hadn't been dashed on the rocks on the way in. But it had become wedged fast between two of them, about half a mile offshore. And that prevented it from sinking. And us from spilling out.

I felt still the boat's motion. My exhausted body bore the memory of it, and I kept staggering from side to side. Now, true it is, I had my sea legs. But I was on shore, where waves broke over and over and the birds flew by or pecked in the sand. Seaweed lay in curves and swirls, like letters of the alphabet, and coming off the ocean was a healthy smell of brine, so different from the appalling stink of the ship. My feeling that I was like to vomit, which had been my constant companion for weeks, had gone, and I was instead ravenously hungry. I took several deep breaths, and gasped as the fresh air hit my lungs.

I felt under my shirt and jerkin, as had become my habit — though on the ship, so as not to cause suspicion, I would pretend to be rubbing my lice. The cipher was still there. Useless it might be, but its presence was a comfort.

Fence and I fell asleep where we landed, on the edge of the water. Fence was sucking the thumb of his gloved hand. I could almost taste the dirty fabric of it in my own mouth, but it didn't seem to bother him. Waking later, thinking I could easily sleep for a hundred years, I glimpsed the smaller outcroppings of rock around our island, which resembled hedgehogs, and watched the clusters of voyagers, still distant on the waves, but approaching.

I began to explore the beach, first having taken off my sodden boots. There hadn't been that much of them to start with, but now they were rotten from long use, brine, and dog shit. My feet were, for the nonce, as bare as Fence's, but I realized it wasn't a comedown. And I was faster without the footwear, which had been flapping around my feet.

Soon I came upon huge sea-land crawlers, very slow, with sleepy blinking eyes that reminded me of Boors. I was a little afraid, but poked one with a stick, whereupon it shut up shop, hiding its head and legs in its horny shell.

"There are legions of insects here," remarked Boors

himself, who had arrived on shore. He sauntered by me, Italian umbrella in hand, as if out for a stroll in town.

Indeed there were. One was creeping up my arm and I knocked it off, leaving a red smear. Winters was close behind Boors, who turned and glared at him.

"I'm in charge now, Spring or Autumn or whatever your name is." Boors laughed triumphantly into Winters' face and put his hand on the admiral's shoulder. "We're on land, and I'm in charge. On behalf of His Majesty. *I am in charge.*"

"We shall see about that," Winters replied grimly.

Boors bowed, his night cap falling onto the sand. The admiral walked on. Boors started to meander along the shore again, but in the other direction. He had left his night cap behind. It was a miracle that despite the storm and his own mangy mindedness, he'd managed to keep it and the umbrella about him all the way to the island.

I ran and put his cap back on his head before watching after him for a moment, but I was soon back to Fence. "The knight and the admiral are at it again."

"It's nothing new, Robin. Winters complains of Boors and Boors complains of Winters daily, and although it's a nuisance and not a good example, it is, I admit, a right welcome change from talk about flies."

"Hm. I hope Winters wins the fight." I had nothing else to say on this subject so I changed it. "Could this be the Isle of Devils?"

"Isle of Devils? I don't know." He was still only half awake. "We shall have to wait for the pilot, with his instruments and measures, to give us our bearings."

Others were landing now, having come in on the ship's small rowboat, which hadn't been jettisoned, or astride empty barrels, or, like us, on wooden planks, part of the ship's carcass. Soon the beach was littered with colonists and crew, many of them asleep. Not Scratcher though. He found me and yanked me up by the ear, as was his wont. Behind him, much to my dismay, stood Proule, his body stuck in a perpetual half bow to Scratcher. I had long hoped him drowned — at least, in an uncharitable corner of my mind.

"My servant at sea and on land," sneered Scratcher, shaking me. "My loyal servant, who threw my comfortable future overboard with my chest."

"Cockroach," muttered Proule, bowing deeper. "Hang him, the dishonest varlet."

"Dishonest? No, sir, not I. Master Thatcher's chest — your chest, Master Thatcher — was taken from me by burly mariners. I would have saved it had I been able." I put on the best look of innocence I could muster. And in truth, I really was innocent. That chest had been at least as important to me as to him.

He cuffed me twice, but changed the subject. "My mouth feels as if it's stuck together with fish glue. Find fresh water, you useless pile, or Proule and I are like to die of thirst."

"Wait, Robin. I'll come with you," called Fence, as I set out across the beach, my feet covered in sand, which thereabouts was pink and fine enough for an hourglass.

"We'll find water, soon enough, I'm sure of it," said I. "And as time goes on, much more."

All manner of jetsam from the ship was already washing up on the shore: wooden planks and ribs, tackling, broken glass, cracked casks, bottles, and spoons. As we walked, I recognized with a thrill of surprise the kerchief I had shoved into the ribs of the hold to stem the leak. It was unmistakable, with its brown and black stripes. Tucking it into my sleeve, I vowed to find its owner and give it back to him.

"Not that he deserves it," said Fence. "He gave you a good shove, as I recall."

"Right. He was a swine. But I can't keep it. I have put the whirr and whoosh of wickedness behind me." And at that moment, scoured clean by the sea and deposited like the jetsam onto the shell pink beach, I truly thought I had.

We continued searching for water in the edges of a spinney with its stands of strange trees, and along the rim of the sea, into which, experience had taught me, fresh rivulets often emptied. But besides a need for water, my belly rumbled mightily for meat. Would there be food here? Would we eat the sea-land crawlers who carried their houses on their backs? I asked Fence whether he thought them eatable.

"Those be tortoises, Robin, or turtles, as some call them. I've seen small ones before. But as to eating one, why, I've never done so."

Could we catch the birds on the beach? They didn't seem in the least afraid of us. One, indeed, had already landed on my shoulder before swooping away. His neck would be easy enough to wring, should he come back, though I felt sick at the thought of doing the deed.

"I can hear the song of your stomach right loud, Robin," said Fence. "But to be honest, mine is singing too."

"Growling, more like." I tapped my noisy belly.

It was then that we saw it, a dark something farther along the shore, having come to rest in front of a rock. It must have been carried along in the wake of the ship, and the tide would have brought it in. My heart thudded as we raced towards it. Could it be? Was it possible? Yes, yes, it was. Just what I had wished and prayed for. Scratcher's sea chest!

Chapter 15

Opening the Chest

The chest was rather the worse for wear, damp and dented and draped in seaweed, but luckily in one piece. And it was still as tightly closed as a clam shell. All thoughts of food vanished from my head, though a crab was crawling over the top of the chest, clicking its pincer.

When I knocked it off it joined some other crabs, which were pursuing a small bird with a broken wing. I felt sorry for the bird, which would soon become crabs' meat, but there was nothing I could do.

I looked around carefully before we moved the chest. There was not a soul nearby, no one to stop us or confide our amazing secret to Scratcher. The voyagers were landing farther down the bay. We could hide the chest in stealth, and visit it at our leisure. But before I returned to my well-worn but risky occupation of pilfering, I had to know whether it might pay off. I sprung the catch, and the lid flew open.

There was a smell of mold and seaweed. Inside the chest, wet and smeared but for the most part whole, were the emblems. Three of them. We would need to separate them and hang them to dry. Somewhere deep in the woods, I thought, on twigs and branches, where no one would find them. I imagined papers and pictures hung out like washing, fluttering in the breeze. We would need to be careful though. Here, quite possibly, was the key to our fortune, returned to us like a ball retrieved by a dog for his master. Now it was only necessary to solve the puzzle. How hard could that be? The first emblem, the one that stupid Scratcher had jettisoned overboard, had already yielded at least some of its secrets.

We lugged the chest into the edge of the spinney. Now I had more leisure, I looked closely at the emblem of the cipher wheel, something I'd never been able to do aboard the *Valentine*. Beneath the emblem was its verse:

> If thou art not by birth or fortune blest
> With means to live or answer thy desire
> With cheerful heart, this cipher doth its best
> To bring to pass the thing thou dost require
> Pay heed to what these emblems really say
> So thou live happy till thy dying day.

I read it out quietly so as not to arouse the suspicion of any who happened to be passing by. I had to clamp my mouth shut to stop myself laughing aloud, but I grinned at Fence. "Look at what it says: *this cipher doth its best to bring to pass the thing thou dost require...*"

"I wonder what that can be."

"Why treasure, treasure of course. There must be treasure hid somewhere. If only this were the place ... the Isle of Devils."

"Perchance it is. But lead us not into temptation," Fence said, although he was grinning right back at me.

Dragging the chest further into the spinney and digging up earth with our hands so we could bury it, at least for the moment, we came upon fresh water, gushings of it. I drank till my belly was full to bursting and tight as a drum; when I moved, I could hear liquid rolling around inside me. Fence had hiccups from drinking too fast. We knew now that we wouldn't die. Not of thirst, anyway, though possibly from drinking too much. We filled a couple of bottles that had washed up on the beach when we'd finished. This was to show that we had done the job Scratcher had sent us to do. Then we moved to a drier spot to bury our booty.

Suddenly there were hoots and hollers, as well as clapping, from further up the shore. Admiral Winters seemed about to speak to the voyagers. Fence and I rushed across, slipping on the wet sand and spilling gobs of water from the bottles, as Winters waited for everyone to gather.

"The pilot tells me we lie in the height of thirty-two-and-a-half degrees of northerly latitude, some two hundred and thirty leagues from Virginia." He paused. "There isn't a sign of the other ships of the fleet and I hope to God they survived. Offer your prayers for the poor souls aboard. But *we* have surmounted the storm, as you know, and are, according to my calculations and the pilot's, safe in the arms of the Bermudas."

"Baruadas?" asked Boors, bleating twice and blinking.

"No, Sir Thomas. The Bermudas."

"The Isle of Devils," the Boatswain said with a low whistle.

Ho Ho.

Chapter 16

Lost in a Dream

We were in the spinney, the trees hung with spider webs big enough to catch birds; huge spiders crouched at their centres. I had been afraid of them at first, but was no longer, as they didn't seem to bite. We were examining the emblems, which we had dried and put back in the chest. We had buried it the second time, well away from the water, with a pattern of stones and twigs over the dirt to show us, but no one else, where it was hid. I put the cipher key inside it too.

For a while we'd been unable to visit, except once quickly, to repack the dried emblems in the chest. Like others, we were busy with the everyday chores of staying alive. We had helped build huts, thatching roofs with wild palm leaves from those strange trees around the shoreline. They looked like feather dusters. The trees of the woods in the forest, more familiar to all, had fashioned the walls of our cabins.

My hands were calloused and sore, and my head ached from the continual cuffings Scratcher gave it. But at least I was alive, something I would never have believed a fortnight since. Of course, I had to live with that tyrant Scratcher. I would rather have stayed with Fence, even in a hut the size of a coal hole. Fence, in his turn, lived with Admiral George Winters, while waiting on Boors and swatting flies for him. There were plenty of real ones to swat now we'd come ashore, along with other fliers, creepers, and crawlers. The bugs were bad. The thought of them made me itch. And indeed, I already had several large bites on my arms and legs that looked like the smallpox. Boors must be in heaven, with so many real insects to grouse about. Or hell.

Today Fence and I had met on the beach.

"Peter Fence!"

"Robin Starveling!"

"Starveling no longer. My belly is stuffed with fowl and tortoises."

"Mine too. And tortoise eggs and fish and crabs. I'm sure I can feel the crabs crawling around inside me. And the voyagers say the crew will roast a pig tonight, to celebrate, as the minister says, our deliverance from the Devil."

"I know. The ship's dog caught it by the leg. The men came running, Boors oinked, and I heard it squeal when stuck."

We laughed at Boors' madness and at the poor pig's demise, although true it is it had made me sick to my stomach when I saw it dispatched. I didn't much care when a man hanged, even if I was obliged to pull on his legs, because he was likely wickeder even than I was and deserved what he got. But I had a soft spot for most animals — except dogs — and hated to see them killed. They'd done nothing wrong. Most of them were as good as I was bad. They were just hanging around minding their own business when someone decided to come calling with a knife to make soup out of them.

Fence hugged me as though we'd not seen each other in years. With one accord, we'd made towards the spinney, where we found the pattern of twigs and stones with difficulty, as some of the markers had vanished, likely in a recent downpour. But find it we did, and dug the chest up again.

"Drag it even deeper into the undergrowth," I bid him, "so nobody sees us."

This was done. Puffing from exertion, we spread the emblems out on the spinney floor, putting a small rock on each to prevent it flying away. They were all a little tattered, as well as quite smudged and brittle from their watery adventure, but their verses were still readable; however, the emblem of the ship, the first emblem I'd found, was of course missing, so although I felt we'd got the gist of it, perchance there was more and we'd never be able to solve the puzzle.

"Mayhap Scratcher lost it," said Fence. "He had it last. Under his shirt."

"He threw it overboard. Didn't I tell you?"

"No. Was he drunk?" Fence looked confused.

"Most likely he was. He certainly is most of the time now. He found two hogsheads of wine washed up, and made me help him roll them along the shore to a clump of rocks and hide them. Every night or two he goes down there to fill his bottle and sometimes Proule's. The ones we found on the shore. He has enough drink for a year at least. And by then he'll have made more. He's experimenting with berries."

"He's right horrible when he's been drinking." Fence frowned at the memory of it.

"Yes. But then again, he's almost as bad sober." My thoughts returned to what we'd been discussing. "He doesn't still have the ship emblem. But even if he had stowed it somewhere, like the wine, it wouldn't have done him much good on its own. 'Go to the Isle of Devils,' it said. Not much else if I recall. And we're here. We're the ones with the other clues … if there are any."

"I'm sure there are, Robin. Where's the cipher key?"

"Here." I took it from the chest. But now, since I'd emerged from the terrors of the tempest, the cipher's pattern of x's and y's had returned to my brain. I knew it backwards and forwards. I'd even dreamed of x's and y's, all in a row, dancing across lines of emblem verse. Dancing daemons. I told Fence about them.

"I've been having some weird dreams myself, of castles and caves, but I put it down to the tortoise eggs, which I *will* eat before bed," he replied. "They're very rich."

"You do know your alphabet, right?" I asked, anxious to get going.

"Aye, but not much more." Fence was staring at the cipher. "Each letter has five x's or five y's or a mix of both next to it."

"Yes."

He was silent for a moment, considering. "It seems to me that it must link up with at least one or two of the emblems, which have letters all over them."

"Mayhap." I wasn't nearly as sure as Fence. "I think the emblem with the cipher wheel has said all it had to say."

"Aye," said my good boy Fence, who usually agreed with me. "But we still have two others. And it's something to do with counting things in fives. I'm good at that."

"You could be right. Mayhap we have to count every five or six x's and y's in the verse to get one letter of the solution." I picked up an emblem. A stand of trees at night with two verses beneath. I picked up another with a picture of the sun, ships, and a rocky beach on it. There was a hand holding a crown in the foreground. The hand was emerging from a cloud. More verses. I scanned it quickly.

"No, this will never work. There aren't enough x's and y's here to make even one word. I can only find one y in these verses altogether. Maybe the pictures mean something … but then, why the cipher wheel? Doesn't it suggest a secret code of some kind? *Pay heed to what these emblems really say.* What they really say, rather than say on the surface?"

Fence shrugged and shook his head. It was growing late. The trees cast ghostly shadows and the tide was coming in. I could hear its dim roar as it broke further and further up the pink sand. It couldn't reach us here though. I suddenly had a prickly feeling, as if Proule or someone else was watching us. I shivered mightily. But it was well-nigh impossible. They were all back at camp.

"You cold, Robin?"

"No, it's just…." And then the strange presence, if that's what it was, vanished. "It's just the night drawing in. There's a coolness to it, giving me goose bumps. I have to go or

Scratcher will beat me blue and black for tardiness. Let's bury the chest somewhere new."

"Deeper in the woods?" asked Fence.

"Yes. For safety. And then, as we go back, we can brood on the meaning of the cipher key."

But true it is, much though we brooded all the way to the cabins, we were no closer to finding a solution to the puzzle. I was beginning to doubt there was one. It was only in the middle of the night that I woke, remembering something peculiar about the verses under the cipher with the hand and crown.

"Ah," cried I, befuddled with sleep and for a moment thinking myself back in the spinney with Fence, "I have it."

"Have wha', huh, you blinking idiot?"

It was Scratcher. His voice was unmistakable though I could certainly smell the wine on him. It was a warm and sickening stench with a hint of vomit to it. Not as bad as Proule though, who smelled *mephitic*, to use one of Ma Oldham's words. I'll give her that, the old witch. She was good for new words, especially nasty ones that sounded much like what they meant. I kept a store of them for every occasion.

There was no moon, and the shutters to our small window hole were closed, making the hut blacker, mayhap, than the night outside. I still couldn't see him, but Scratcher's voice came through the dark so curdled with drink that the end sounds were falling off his words. "Have wha'?" he repeated.

"Uh." I thought fast. "My kerchief, Master Scratcher. That is, Master Matchett's kerchief, but when I get a ghost of a chance I mean to...." I came to a full stop. I'd returned it weeks before, and Matchett had offered to shake hands with me.

"You're a filthy worsted-stocking knave, you know tha'?"

"No, sir."

"God's Blood! Lucky I can't see you or I'd knock you into Sunday."

"But it's only Tuesday now, sir."

"Shut your bloody trap and go back to slee'."

"I shall, sir, never fear." I cradled my head in my hands lest he take it into his drunken brain to come after me in the dark and wallop me there and then, not wait for Sunday at all.

In the morning I recalled waking in the night, but my brain had totally misplaced the cipher solution. Mayhap it had only been the product of a dream. When I told Fence he said that doubtless my conversation with Scratcher had been part of the dream too, or nightmare, more like, induced by too much eating of the roast pig and the fishes that accompanied it. He reminded me of several other good or bad dreams I'd had. He could have been right. Though if this one *had* been a nightmare, it had certainly sounded and smelled like the real sheep-shit Scratcher.

CHAPTER 17

DECIPHERING!

All day I'd been trying to think up solutions. But "that won't work; that won't work either," I kept muttering to myself. I felt that if I didn't get the answer soon, I'd go completely mad. On pretense of fetching wood for a cooking fire, I'd come back to the spinney to look at the hand from the clouds emblem and see if it would remind me of what I'd forgotten, but I'd only got the chest half dug out when I heard a noise. That devil Proule and some of the other men, including Stephen Beerson, clerk to the minister of a Sunday, were speaking to one another in hushed tones a few yards away, hidden, no doubt purposely, in the undergrowth. Trusty and Ruffles were there too. I could tell by their voices. And there were glimpses of Mary's tattered red skirt through the bushes and trees. I was surprised she was there. She must have healed her rift with Proule.

"That could get us all killed," I heard someone say. "I'm leaving now." It was one of the crew. He broke into a run as he left, a fearful look on his face. He passed so close that I couldn't believe he didn't notice me, but mayhap he was too upset.

What could they be discussing? I covered the chest with earth and scaled a cedar as silently as I could, its feathery needles crushing under my hands. I'd always been a good tree climber. It was almost a necessity for a felon such as myself. It put me, in a manner of speaking, above the law. From way up on a bough I could look down on Proule and his remaining cohorts without being observed, and that suited me, you might say, down to the ground.

"It can't get us killed. We have authority backing us," said Mary, which made me even more curious.

"So we're agreed then," Proule said to Mary and the fellows.

"We're agreed. Roberts there-gone is a fool and a coward," said Trusty.

"Right," agreed Ruffles. They always agreed with each other.

"Aye, we're agreed, Praise the Lord, every man of us," said Beerson.

"And woman too." This, of course, was Mary.

"Swear most solemnly, that we'll do what he wants, on God's name."

They laid their hands atop one another's, palm down. "We swear."

"On God's name," added Beerson, who didn't take his duties lightly.

"On God's name," the others dutifully repeated. Then they were gone, slipping like wraiths through the woods and to our settlement, so as not to draw attention to themselves. I slid down the tree slowly. The crew man had shown by leaving that they were likely up to something, probably no good. And that *someone* — I didn't know who — wanted them to do *something* — I didn't know what. That scared but excited me. Yet another mystery for Fence and me to unravel!

Fence was coming towards me now, his hose hitched above his knees, pale face sprinkled with freckles birthed in the hot sun of the Bermudas. "You smell of cedars."

"The smell must have rubbed off on me. I was up a tree."

"Let's take another look at those emblems," he said.

"Right-o, but I have to piss first." I would keep the news of what I'd seen till later.

We relieved ourselves, sniggering with embarrassment as we did so. It was so different from the boat. The spinney being large and uncrowded, save for the trees, made it all more personal somehow, than if everyone in the hold was pissing in a pail together. Afterwards we pulled up our hose, or rather what was left of it, holes held together by threads, and returned to the more serious business of looking again at the emblem: a hand holding a crown as it emerged from the clouds. It was Fence who came upon the first real bit of evidence for the cipher, because, as luck would have it, he was such a poor reader. He could put words together slowly and painfully, but he said himself that it took him most of daylight to read a sentence.

"Let me read it, let me read it, Robin," he begged. I agreed reluctantly, as I was impatient, but this would be, after all, an aid to the boy's education. He took the paper from me so he could pore over it more closely, but he soon came unstuck.

"I can't read the whole line," he said.

"Of course you can," I encouraged, like a good teacher. "Spell it out."

"A" he started. "That's the whole of the word because then there's a gap. Just A."

"Yes, good."

"S-E-C-R-E-T … se … cret."

"Right." I was becoming impatient. Impatience made me itchy. I began to rub my bites.

"A again — can't read the next letter."

I was getting really annoyed. At this rate we'd never solve anything. I looked over his shoulder at the emblem. "Surely you can. You just saw it in 'secret.'"

"No I didn't."

"Yes you did. It's an R."

Perhaps I was doing wrong in trying to teach him. Likely he was as unteachable with letters as I was with numbers, though he was a quick thinker in other ways. I read the line aloud, tired of waiting: "*A secret arm stretched out from the sky....*" This hinted at a mystery all by itself. I felt, as my blood rushed to my throat, that we were on the right track.

"No it's not an R. Not like any R I've ever seen. And there are other funny letters too."

"Don't be daft. Give it here." I read the entire verse quickly:

> A secret arm stretched out from the sky,
> In double chain a diadem doth hold,
> Whose circlet bounds the greater Britanny,
> From conquered France, to England sung
> of old...

"It's about kings," said Fence wonderingly.

"Yes. Kings of England."

I looked at the emblem again. And then I realized. The verse was laid out in two kinds of letters. One kind that Fence could read, and one that he couldn't. The second R of the line didn't look like the first, it was much more elaborate. That was a problem for Fence, but as an experienced reader, I could decipher each. Those he couldn't read, though, the ones in what that old crone Oldham would call "secretary script," were harder for me too.

"Fence," I said importantly, picking a couple of lice off my head and sticking them in my mouth, an old habit, "you're going to have to help me count letters. I believe I have the answer. It's simple."

"It is?"

"Yes. You gave it to me by accident. There are two kinds of writing in this emblem, though I don't think there were in the ship emblem. Letters in one kind are x's. Letters in the other are y's. We have to count off the letters in the verse in fives. That will be your job. And then we'll see how many x's and y's are in each counted off section, and match each section to a letter of the alphabet in the cipher key."

Fence looked completely lost. There was a small stick next to me, and I picked it up, scratching letters out in the dirt. "Every five letters in the emblem verse equals one letter of the secret message. D'you see? So if we have five letters in a row in the 'x' writing, that would be an A, because the cipher says that A equals xxxxx. And if we have four letters in a row in the 'x' writing, followed by a letter in the 'y' writing, we have a B, because the cipher says that B equals xxxxy. Get it now?"

"I'm just beginning to." Fence scratched his head as if he wasn't. "Show me more."

"Here." I wrote the beginning of the emblem verse, counting very carefully.

A secr/et a*r*m/e
A   C

"You could read the first five letters of the verse. Therefore they're all x's. Five x's in a row are an A, according to the cipher key. You could read the next three letters too, e-t-a, but couldn't read the r. So that's xxxy. Can you read the next letter?"

"Aye, it's an m." He still looked perplexed.

"So that's an x too. Do you see? In other words the next five letters read xxxyx. That's a C according to the cipher. So we have the first two letters of the solution: A C.

Fence pored over the emblem for at least two minutes. "I understand, Robin, I understand," he exclaimed at last, clapping his hands.

"Good. You're the better counter. You'll do the counting."

"Aye. Let's do the rest now."

True it is, there was nothing I wanted to do more. But the sun was already tipping down from the zenith and turning the colour of an orange. I'd been away for hours. "We'll work on it tomorrow."

"Please, can't we just do another letter or two?"

But I'd already stood up, and was dusting down my sleeves and hose. "Can't. Even though I want to. Have to pick up some wood for a fire and get back or Scratcher will knock me into Sunday, so he says." I was already packing up emblems and lugging the chest back to the hole we'd taken it from.

Fence stood by sadly, chewing his nails, which were as filthy as my own.

"Help me cover this," I said. We pushed dirt into the hole, ran back to the settlement and separated. After looking around to make sure no one was watching, I nicked an armful of wood that was piled outside someone else's hut and hurried with it to Scratcher's.

It was only then that I remembered Proule and his cohorts. I'd been so elated at solving the cipher, I'd forgotten completely to tell Fence about the secret meeting.

Inside, Scratcher and Proule were drinking and arguing about something that had to do with Boors' idiot madness and his inability to govern the settlement or even himself.

"Where you been all this time?" Scratcher demanded, his face surly as he turned from Proule.

"Out collecting sticks for the fire, master, as I told you. They're piled outside. It was work and a half, I can tell you."

"Hmph. You better be telling the truth."

"I am, sir."

"More wine," said Proule loudly, holding up his bottle.

Scratcher held up his own. "Serve us, you lousy whelp of a mongrel." Picking up both bottles, exhausted as I was, I hastened along the beach to fetch more drink from Scratcher's stash in the rocks. At this rate it would run out much faster than I'd calculated.

"I know a secret," slurred Proule after another swig or

two. Scratcher, who had been scratching his unmentionables, as usual, stopped for a minute.

"A secret?" he asked.

"Aye, but I'm not telling yer, Bill Scratcher."

"The name is William Thatcher, you gas-ridden ape. God's Blood! Tell me the goddamn secret."

"Not ruddy likely. And I ain't no ape. Watch yer mouth, Scratcher, or I'll watch it for yer."

They were going at it again. I slunk into the corner shadows, realizing unhappily that there would be no supper this day. It was too late to fish for it myself and Scratcher had been too lazy to cook or fetch even a tortoise egg. But there was still the possibility of a secret passed from one to the other. I tried not to sleep. I tried to listen hard to them as they shouted, sang, and fought through the night. I was hoping that the secret might slip out. But unless I did fall to dreaming and miss something important, Proule was true to his word. He didn't so much as whisper of secret doings. And in the end they were so roaring drunk that they threw punches at each other and swore the other had stolen their goods, emblems, boxes, and wine, till the air turned blue.

There was something about the Isle of Devils that seemed to make every man the enemy of every other, although true it is that Scratcher and Proule, even if partners of a sort, had made a fine start on their quarrels before they even set foot on land. It had happened to them. It had happened to Boors and Winters, who went at it hammer and tongs. I crossed my fingers, hoping it wouldn't happen to Fence and me. In any event, Proule threw one last threat at Scratcher and left. Scratcher took out his knife and waved it at Proule's retreating back. Then he fell headlong onto the floor, missing his own knife blade by an inch at most, and started to snore.

Chapter 18

In the Spinney

The next time I managed to escape I met up with Fence, whose master was more lenient about his comings and goings. In the spinney I had him count off the emblem verse in fives. His tongue tip hung a little out of his mouth in concentration. When he'd done, I began to solve the cipher.

"A crown," I said triumphantly. "That's how it begins."

"A crown? Is this a *royal* secret?" His eyes were round as apples.

"Perchance. That would be in accord with the words of the verse themselves." The ship's dog had lolloped up to us wagging his tail cautiously. His tongue hung out a bit too. I shoved him away. He whined a bit but returned.

"What comes next?" Fence was patting him.

"Stop that, Fence, for mercy's sake, or the beast will never go elsewhere."

Fence gave him a last pat. "I don't mind if he doesn't. Don't forget, he trapped that pig for all of us. Shoo, Tempest," he went on, without any conviction.

"Tempest"?

"That's what I've named him: Tempest, in honour of the storm. He had no name except 'Dog' before." The animal lolled against him, before trotting over to a nearby tree and cocking a leg.

"Hmm. I guess he can't give away our cipher." I turned back to the verse. "This is harder than Oldham's stupid lessons." I rotated the page a couple of times. "At."

"Aye?"

"This would be much easier if I had a slate to write things down on," I grumbled.

"Use the sand, like you did before."

I scribbled in the dirt with a rather thorny stick, while Fence fidgeted and sucked the tip of his thumb, as was his wont. "The end," I said finally, after wrestling with the letters, especially the secretary hand. I was very tired.

"The end? But we've hardly begun. Don't give up now."

I sighed. "No, "the end" is part of the message: 'The crown at the end…."

"The end of what? The end of what?"

"Shh. Let me take another look." I stared and scribbled in the sand, stared and scribbled some more. The sun rose high in the sky and beat down on us between the leaves. The words jumped up on down on the page. I began to sweat.

"'Of the path.' Yes, true it is, 'The crown at the end of the path.' That's the whole message," I crowed, victorious at last. This was exciting. I had actually solved something. I imagined a great glittering crown on a beautiful pathway bordered by flowers. I waited for Fence to offer his congratulations.

"The path? What path?"

Elation drained out of me. "Well, how the hell should I know? We're in the right place, Devil's Island, according to the other emblem, so we'll have to look for it. Perhaps it even begins in the woods here. But we can't look today. I'm too tired. Scratcher kept me up all night, yammering and fighting with his henchman." That reminded me. I still hadn't told Fence about Proule and Mary.

I lay down on the spinney floor and shut my eyes. Even so, I could still see light and dark, light and dark, shimmering across my eyelids as the sun patchworked through the canopy of the trees. And that blasted dog Tempest had lain down next to me. I could feel his hot breath against my side and hear little panting noises and grunts, but was too exhausted to do anything about it. I opened one eye, saw a black floppy ear standing straight up in the air and a white one pointing straight down. It gave the beast a quizzical expression, as if he were saying, "What's this knave about to do to me now?" I was about to do nothing. I couldn't even imagine lifting my hand to push him away, but I didn't need to. In a single blink he had gone, chasing after a lizard. I shut my eye again. And slept.

"Put the verse away and shut the chest," I commanded when I awoke, as if Fence were my servant, in the same way that I was Scratcher's. "Cover it with earth. Commit the message to memory, as I will, and wipe out what's on the dirt. And then I have something to tell you about Proule."

"Proule?"

I opened both eyes. "Hell's Bells, Fence, stop repeating everything I say or I'll go completely barmy. Yes, Proule. And Mary, his old enemy. And others." That was a huge puzzle too. And one about to burst open like an overripe plum, suggested the small wicked voice in my ear.

Plums. I rubbed a new mosquite bite as I thought about them. I'd pilfered plenty off the barrows in Plymouth in the past. And now I'd had no supper, nor no breakfast either, and there wasn't a barrow nor shop in sight. I could almost taste the soft sweetness of the absent plums, though I remembered the pain when one got stuck on the way down when it wasn't ripe enough. Ouch. But now even an unripe plum was out of the question, though I was starved and ready to put up with anything.

When Fence had finished his tasks, I scrambled up and we went to look for molluscs in the confusion of rocks and sea at the shore. The tide was coming in, spraying the rocks, and we paddled our toes in the eddies. I told Fence what I'd seen and heard the day before, and his forehead creased. "A conspiracy?"

"It's possible." I shrugged. I liked to think that much of my devilry had been washed clean away by the roar and whine of the sea storm. But now, true it is, having seen Proule and Mary and the others in the woods, I wanted a stake in any wickedness that might occur. My heart beat faster, my brain urged it, though I tried hard not to admit my interest even to myself. And I shouldn't even mention wickedness to Fence, I realized, who was still young, and straight and clean as an arrow. Or at least, so I liked to think. I said no more on the subject.

After eating a snail-like creature or two, which slunk down my gullet and comforted my belly, I commenced looking for the emblem path with Fence, who wouldn't leave off nagging. We searched the rest of the day in the woods, our legs sorely prickled by thorns and sharp grass. The wind was still. The sun slanted through the trees and spider webs, its brilliant yellow slats spearing the ground at intervals as if to guide us. The tide finished coming in, and started going out. But we found nothing. Mayhap the path was overgrown. Or mayhap it had never been there in the first place. It was a bafflement.

Chapter 19

Storm Sighting

The ocean was beginning to roar. Rain spat and then, with little warning, poured from clouds. Lightning rent the welkin as ants ran for cover and we ran for home. Just before we reached the settlement we caught sight of three shadowy forms half hidden by a large rock. They stood very close to each other, close enough to be telling a secret.

"Is that Admiral Winters?" I asked, sodden from head to foot.

"Looks to be him. And Proule. Who's the other?"

Jagged lightning lit the three figures, followed by an ear-splitting stroke of thunder. "Why, Fence, good fellow, don't you see?" I blinked hard, trying to clear my eyes of rain. "A ragged red skirt, hair longer than the admiral's. There stands Mary Finney, bold as brass. That witch gets into everything."

"At least there's three of them so they can't be a-lying down together," Fence said seriously, wiping his face.

"True it is." I laughed, but wondered what Mary wanted with Winters and Proule. No answer occurred to me, unless she was eager to tittle-tattle about a fourth person, perhaps Scratcher. Or me. At that moment she passed us by, hurrying back to the cabins, her hair plastered to her head and neck. The two men had disappeared.

"What you looking at, stupid?" she asked.

"Not you, Mary, Mary Fish-Finney. Not you."

"You just remember that, toad spawn. You ain't seen no one." She had been with Proule, that vicious beast, and Winters, the real power of the settlement in spite of that title going to Boors, so she was confident. Whatever she'd been doing with them, she was safe. Fence and I waited for a moment before following the same trail back.

I finally reached Scratcher's and shoved several baked eggs, leftover from lunch, down my throat. I peeled and ate so fast that one got stuck, and I had to choke it back up. Afterwards I slid into my habitual corner, still too drenched and chilled to sleep. Mary, Winters, Proule, I whispered to myself over and over again as I tried to rub myself warm. Fish Fin, Winter Nights, Cat Pee. And occasionally, as I finally began to nod off, xxyyx, yyxxy. Scratcher, Heaven be praised, was in a drunken stupor, crying and mumbling about his lost chest and his lost treasure. If he only knew....

Chapter 20

They're Gone!

There was much alarmed talk. The admiral had disappeared several days before. So had Proule. So had Salt-fish Mary, though no one took much notice of that. Others were missing from the settlement too, including the men I'd seen in the spinney speaking to Proule. And though I'd searched everywhere, I couldn't find Peter Fence. That was most alarming of all. He had melted into thin air. I knew he wouldn't leave me, not willingly anyhow. I was all he had in the way of comfort in the world. He must have been forcibly taken. Or worse, drowned.

Boors was more demented than usual. With Fence doing a disappearing act, he had no one to swat flies for him. He slapped his legs and arms continuously while calling for the boy in a quavering voice. Within a day he'd lost both his nightcap and his umbrella. Piggsley, who had made a fly swatter out of twigs, was obliged to help him out. Others were more concerned with practical matters.

"With the admiral and half the crew gone," said an exhausted-looking colonist, "how will we ever reach Jamestown?" Half the crew was a bit of an exaggeration, but at least we got his point. Now we had only the lunatic Boors to lead us. And Boors would be incapable of stepping out of a wooden bucket on his own, never mind anything else.

"I have to get to Virginia," yelled Scratcher, as the news sunk into his sotted brain. "I'm to be secretary."

No one was listening to him. He wasn't secretary yet. They were arguing with one another about what was best to be done.

"We should go out and search for 'em," said a mariner.

"We should stay put and let them get on with it. More food for us," said another, rubbing his belly.

"Why must we leave here?" asked a small girl in a small voice. "I don't want to go back on the sea."

"There's enough food to keep us all full. I'm for staying on this island forever," said one of the colonists.

"I'm to be secretary of the colony, I say," Scratcher screeched, his face purple.

"There won't be enough food. Not come winter."

"Rot, there's plenty of food for all," replied another voyager, ignoring Scratcher altogether. He glared around as if daring someone to contradict him.

Scratcher screeched again, like a drunken monkey. The

wind was beginning to rise and there was a scent of rain and wine.

"Little Lettis has said true. We're likely better off here on Devil's Island than goin' awa' over to Virginia, anyway, which Winters will make us do if he comes hither again."

"Right," agreed someone else, pulling his tatty cape around him. "God knows what awaits us on the seas, never mind Jamestown."

A young woman began to cry. "I hate this Isle of Devils."

"Me too," whined a little boy with a dead crab in his hand.

"I heard tell the admiral was building a pinnace. Perhaps they be already gone. My intended be in Jamestown. Now I never will see him again."

The pilot arrived. "Who's missing in addition to the admiral?"

"Michael Angel, for one…."

"No, I've just seen him."

"Mortimer Proule is gone."

"Who cares? We're better off without the old sod."

"Secretary of the colony…." moaned Scratcher.

"Shut up!" yelled the pilot. Scratcher shut up.

Other voices were rising and vanishing into the wind, and people were shoving one another. It was beginning to pour with rain, cold and hard, as it had done all this week. They would never come to agreement. They would never do anything. They had, in fact, forgotten they were talking about Winters and were fighting with each other over nothing of importance at all.

I felt desolate and lonely but wasn't about to give up. Creeping into our hut behind Scratcher, who had finally given up his claims of grace and favour, at least for the moment, I thought, as I warmed my bones somewhat, about what I might or could accomplish in the light of this new mystery. Not in the interests of wickedness, for once, but of friendship. I missed my boy Fence. The next afternoon, with the wintry sun streaming through the trees, I was back in the spinney searching for clues.

I looked on the ground for footprints, but the rain had scrubbed everything clean. I gazed at the bark of cedars, thinking that Fence might have scratched some kind of clue, and into the lacy, leafy canopy. I widened my search to the pink sand of the beach, and I examined the limpet rocks. Everything was as usual. Everything was empty of evidence. Sitting down in damp grass by the shore, I rubbed my head hard until at last, as the day began to darken, an idea popped into it. I went back into the deeps of the tall Bermuda forest, where the trees grew wild and private, as a bird swooped down and perched on my shoulder. Carefully, I uncovered the top of the chest, and sprung open the lid, afraid that I would find nothing. The bird flew away.

Nothing, nothing, I repeated to myself. I will find nothing.

But lo and behold, Fence's old black glove, never before

separated from his right hand, was waiting inside. It was stuffed with palm leaves and its fingers pointed south, towards a stretch of water. Not to Virginia, which lay to the west. They hadn't gone there. Oh, my clever Fence, I hurrahed to myself. Not a book learner or even a writer of the alphabet, to be sure, but no fool either. He had shown me the way. I would paddle south, across the watery expanse, to the next island, an island I had never ventured to explore before. But that's where Winters and Proule and Finney and the others went, dragging Fence along with them, I was sure of it now. I left the glove in the chest, and read the verse of the last unsolved emblem over and over till I knew it. Then I stuffed it under my jerkin. I would sail on the tide of tomorrow, and try to solve the cipher before I went.

CHAPTER 21

HELLISH HEAD BANG

On the ground. Just woken up, but still very drowsy. Godawful headache, like I'd been knocked over the head with a rock. I fell asleep again, for a few minutes or maybe more. When I awoke, I had sand in my mouth. I could taste blood in it. And there was a bad smell. I'd pissed in my hose. I turned over and felt around my head with two fingers. It was wet, but not from the sea. The wetness felt sticky and warm. Blood or brains were leaking out. I opened one eye for a second then shut it tight against the sun, which was searing. Something was licking the stickiness on my head. I was too tired to raise my arm again and push it away. I was too tired and headachey to reopen my eyes. I hoped to hell it was the ship's dog and not some ferocious beast. Maybe Tempest had swum over too.

Memory returned slowly. I'd left our island, having told only Piggsley goodbye. "I s'd come with you, Ginger

Top, if I could," he said, giving me a pat on the shoulder. I reckoned he wouldn't give me away, and I felt I needed to have someone in the know just in case I disappeared for good. So I wouldn't vanish from the face of the earth with no one to notice my passing. But when I told him I was going, he immediately asked me. "Who s'll I tell, lad, if you goes missing?"

I had none who cared over in England should I vanish. And no one here except him. "Nobody, Master Piggsley, nobody at all."

I fleetingly wondered whether I should say he might inform Mistress Oldham of Plymouth Town, but dismissed the idea as soon as it bubbled into my brain. "Good riddance to stinking rubbish," she would likely respond, her idea of a fitting epitaph.

He walked me down to the shore and shook my hand like a gentleman, calling me a good soul. "And if we be'ant to meet agin in this life," he said, "we s'll meet in the next, never fear."

I hand paddled over to the island south and slightly west of ours. The wind was high so I bent low, gripping the broad plank I rode on between my knees. Piggsley and I had found the plank, washed up from the *Valentine*, on the shore. Sprays of salt water drenched me as I went. The sea got into my mouth and I choked on it. Coughing, I fell off the plank. I scrabbled around for it, but it was already behind me, swept back by the waves, so I had to swim to the island, which was still a long way off. The tide was pulling me the other way. My clothes were dragging me under. I wrenched off my jerkin and the emblem went with it, down into the depths. Lucky I'd solved it. There was no way I could dive after it. My arms were too painful from all the paddling and swimming. I was close to drowning. Tempest the dog had swum up behind me. He barked twice, as if to urge me on, and pushed me once, with his paw.

I made it to shallow water, scrambled up and waded to the land. Sobbing with exhaustion and effort, I gasped land air into my lungs. I could see smoke, no doubt the smoke of a cooking fire, further inland. So perhaps they were here then, Winters and his crew. They or someone else. I was creeping towards the sight and smell of the smoke when I was smacked hard from behind, and went out like a snuffed candle. Even Oldham's frying pan over the head routine had nothing on this. As I fainted, I heard someone screaming. Perchance it was me.

Now I still felt weird, half asleep. I tried to think about the cipher in the final emblem. For a moment I couldn't remember what it said or even what the emblem verse was. The plain text. Or the picture. I was too confused. Why would I even think about ciphers at such a time anyway? It was a kind of madness. But I did think about it, I couldn't help myself, and its words and meaning were slowly coming back to me. I could almost see letters set out on the parchment. Not all of them though. I couldn't recall all of them.

I managed to open both eyes before squinting around. Everything was hazy. Two figures loomed above me, huge and dark against the sun. Perhaps they were the wild men talked of in England. The wild men of the New World. Or Spaniards. Either way, they'd likely kill me. I banged my eyes shut and pretended to be dead. Mayhap, I thought, I already am, and this is hell. But at that moment I realized with relief that they were speaking English. Then with dread, because one of them was Proule. I could tell by his voice.

"What you do to him?" asked the other voice.

"I hit 'im. Hard. He went down like a slit pig," retorted Proule.

"He's Scratcher's boy."

"I know that. He ain't supposed to be here. He could rat us all out. I ain't wanting to see Scratcher's face again ever in this life, not after our last set-to. I ain't wanting to see him again even after, if we're both sent below."

"Below?"

"To ruddy Hades."

"Is the boy dead?"

"I'll find out." Proule kicked me hard in the side. I moaned, staggered up, then fell onto both knees, my head spinning. The dog stood nearby, looking a bit stunned. Proule kicked him too. He yelped and cringed, before running over to me. I was too hurt to reach out, but felt a sudden and unfamiliar kinship with him. Tempest. Good dog. *Pax vobiscum*. Peace be with you.

"Nope," Proule went on. "Starveling's not dead. He reeks like dead fish but he ain't dead." I was amazed he could smell me over his own noisome stench. But perchance he was so used to his own stink that he thought he smelled like attar of roses. "In point o'fact," Proule went on, "he's alive."

"That's lucky," said the other man.

"Aye, that's lucky. That's good news." Proule sounded as if it wasn't. "On yer feet, cockroach," he shouted, loud enough to deafen me. He dragged me up by the ear. "I'm taking yer to the gov'nor and making a present out of yer for him."

He punched me in the back to help me get going. Feeling as if my spine had cracked in two, I screamed again.

"Shut yer yap," Proule shouted.

A small crowd, no doubt alerted by my shrieks and Proule's yelling, was already gathering. I recognised people: Mary Finney, Stephen Beerson, the minister's clerk, Sam Buyers and Abraham Carpenter, sailors both, and Admiral Winters himself, who I supposed to be the gov'nor. There were some others. I didn't see Peter Fence anywhere, but true it is that my right eye was very sore, that's the side of the head where Proule had bashed me, and I couldn't look leftwards.

Proule let go of my ear and I sank to the ground.

"What's this? What's this?" asked the admiral.

"It's Scratcher's boy, Admiral Winters."

"I can see that. How did he get that gash on his head?"

"I give it him, knowing he'd come to spy." Proule picked up a heavy stick, probably *the* stick, and pantomimed hitting me for Winters.

"Put the stick down, Proule." Winters face was stern. He would brook no nonsense.

After a further swish or two of it to show he wasn't bested, Proule complied.

"Spy?" asked Winters now, with a curl of the lips.

"Aye, sir. He's a right crooked little cockroach, full of tricks like that. He should be hanged high, sir. Hanged high. Wouldn't take me more'n a minute. I've suggested it before, but to no avail." He didn't know how true that was. He spat into his hands and rubbed them together briskly. "He should be hanged high, admiral," he repeated a third time, as though he relished the words.

He was serious. I gasped. If there was anything worse than drowning, it was being hanged. I'd seen enough of it, and pulled enough dangling legs to know.

"What's your name, boy?" asked Winters.

"Robin Starveling, sir." I struggled to get up. "I haven't come to spy. I was missing my good friend Peter Fence and came to find him."

"Perhaps we should send you back to Master Thatcher, should we?"

"No sir. Please sir, anything but that. Master Thatcher is not a good master. I'd rather serve you. And I want to stay with Peter Fence, if he" — I crossed my fingers — "if he is here."

"He *is* here. He is out collecting logs for the fire."

"Best to hang this boy, I say. Hang him an' quarter him and cut him up for swine swill. Them pigs'll eat anything. He's Scratcher's creature, so he must be up to no good." Proule picked up the stick again and twirled it twice before throwing it high, high, in the air. It dropped into the sea, but there were plenty of others around.

"Am I to die?" I whispered, my lips almost frozen with fear.

"No boy, you are not," said Winters. "Neither of your injuries, which we will take care of, nor by hanging."

"Send the blighter back," yelled Mary Finney. "Since you ain't going to hang him. We don't need the likes of him here. And send that vicious animal Proule back while you're at it." So her quarrel with Proule wasn't fixed after all. Not entirely, at least.

"I've seen the boy with Peter Fence before; they are friends, as Starveling said, and that is no bad thing in these terrible times. I shall take into account what Fence has to say before deciding whether to keep the boy or send him back to Boors and Thatcher."

"Yer take a cabin boy's chuntering over my own word that this here cockroach is a fool and a spy who will spoil our good government?"

"I do," replied Winters. "Even if the young man were a spy, which I doubt, I fear nothing from him. He cannot harm us. Sir Thomas and I agreed to part and each govern our own domain."

"So yer says."

"I am in charge here, and I will brook no disobedience from you. In fact, Proule, looking at your handiwork this day, I wish to God I had never brought you to this place. Mary has a point."

As I lay there watching them, I wished Winters hadn't brought Mary either. She was sporting a nasty expression. Proule, meanwhile, stood his ground sullenly, but he said not a word as Winters beckoned to two men in the crowd. "You there, sirrahs. Bear the boy to camp. Gently."

Stephen Beerson and Sam Buyers lifted me. Beerson slid his fingers under my arms, his nails digging into my armpits. He was praying in a dark mumble, hopefully for my recovery. Buyers grabbed my knees. He was swearing, but not loud enough for Winters to hear, about how I weighed more than a sackful of turnips, and if he had to carry anything he'd rather it be the turnips. At least he could eat them after. The wound in my head brushed against Beerson's chest as the two men hoisted me. I dragged my hand up and stuffed it into my mouth to keep from screaming again.

The crowd was beginning to disperse. But Mary stood stock still, glaring at me as the mariners carried me by. Proule, cheated of a hanging, the hanging of someone he clearly wanted rid of, made a gargoyle of his face, not that he wasn't ugly enough to begin with. He spat again, but into the sand this time. I knew he would have spat on me directly, and perchance have done much worse, had Winters not been there to curb him. He was not only angry. He was humiliated, which made him even more dangerous. Sick and in pain as I was, I felt evil rising inside me like a foul black tide. I felt reckless. I wanted him dead.

Chapter 22

Eating and Telling Tales

"What I wouldn't give for a trencher of hot porridge," I told Fence a few days later.

"You're feeling better then, Robin? Thanks be that you are. You haven't taken a bite of food in three days. In fact, you've barely been awake, though you've been spouting rubbish."

"What kind of rubbish?"

"I don't rightly know. I could hardly make it out to be English. It made no sense to my ears and was all mashed together like the filling of a mince tart."

"A word pudding," I said. That reminded me of food once more. "I'd give a shilling — that's if I had one — for a plate of mashed neeps. Or a Shrovetide pancake sodden with butter and honey. Or an entire apple pie in its pastry coffin, with raisins and spice."

"You *are* feeling better!"

"Yes, Fence, my boy, I am. I'm starving. The devilish pounding in my head has stopped. I still feel sore, though, where that monster kicked and punched me."

"Aye, Robin. Monster he is, right enough; sadly for you he was on shoreline duty that day you came in. But the admiral has told him off, good and proper. He'd be mad to lay into you again."

At that moment I noticed Fence's right hand for the first time — the first time, that is, without his glove. He had suffered the largest and most terrible gash sometime in the past. The scar looked like a big S. "What happened to your hand?" I asked.

"Nothing." He hid it behind his back.

"I never pushed you before about it. But we're friends. You can tell me."

"It is a story I do not like to tell, and that's why I've always worn a glove. It's a pity you couldn't bring it with."

"It's still in the chest. We'll collect it when we go back, *if* we go back. Now tell me. Please."

"Aye, I feel right silly about it, but I will." He brought his hand forward and stared at it as he spoke. "When my father died, my mother married another man, John Shepherd. He was cruel with me, Robin, right enough, and hated the fact I was another man's son. Every week he would ask the same question. 'What is your name, boy?' and every week I would answer, 'My name is Peter Fence, sir.' One day, when he was angry beyond reason because one of our dogs, which he'd beaten, had died, he said to me, 'You're not his anymore. You belong to me.' He went and fetched a dagger and carved a long S on my hand. I suppose it stood for Shepherd. My mother cried, but did nothing, as she was very afraid of him too. I got a fever from the cut, but no one tended me. As soon as I healed, I ran away to sea. I've never seen my family since."

He paused, but I stayed silent, unable to think of anything to say. I wasn't shocked. How could I be, having grown up in a world of cruelty myself? Scratcher had threatened me with a knife, after all. And he wasn't the first, by any means. And I'd been whipped and beaten many a time. But I felt very, very sorry for Fence, who said nothing about the horrible pain he must have endured.

"I thought it would fade and disappear, but instead, as my hand grew bigger, it stretched and grew bigger too." Fence looked shamed and hid his hand behind his back again.

"You've nothing to be ashamed of, Peter Fence, and you certainly shouldn't feel silly. You should wear the scar as a badge of courage and honour."

"Thank you, Robin. You are my family now."

I wanted to respond in kind, but was unused to talking in such a way. I didn't remember having either family or friends before. We sat quietly for a while, but soon I heard the sound of hammering, and roused myself enough to look around. We were under some kind of lean-to to protect us from the weather. Its back was resting against a large fallen cedar. The front, which slanted to the ground, was covered with slats made of branches, but through the open triangle at the side I could see men erecting huts, thatching roofs from palm leaves, and walling in wild pigs that wanted to be walled *out*. Tempest was barking at them and wagging his tail at the same time. Mary, sleeves rolled up, was roasting birds on a spit over a fire. Proule, thanks be, was not visible. Lying in wait behind a different cedar, mayhap. I shuddered. But for the moment anyway, the scene looked very peaceful and countrified. *Bucolic*, ratbag Oldham would call it, with an air of disdain. She was a town ratbag through and through. She looked down on country ratbags.

Fence was back to the subject of food. "We have some turtle eggs, raw still, or I could beg you a leg of plover from Mary. I'll say it's for me."

I nodded at the mention of plover. I didn't think I could manage another turtle egg as long as I lived. The very thought of them raw, round and soft with watery whites and yolks spilling out of their papery cases, turned me queasy all over again.

Fence was soon back. He crept, doubled over, through the side opening. "Her red skirt was filthy, greasy with bird fat," he reported. "What with that and the holes, she looks right bad. And she was talking to herself in what might have been Irish. But she gave a leg to me."

"Not one of her own, I hope." I grinned painfully. Fence laughed. After gnawing the plover leg, taking a long draft of water, and crawling outside the lean-to to piss, I was onto more important business. "Tell me your story, Fence."

"What story would that be, Robin?"

"The story of how you came to be here on this island with Winters and the others. Before, I was too ill to ask."

"There's not much to tell. The admiral and Boors were fighting all the time, and the admiral couldn't stand Boor's stupidity one whit longer. He wanted his own command. So he built a small boat, a pinnace, with some of his crew and sundry others, and came across here to live, despite Boors saying he was in charge. The boat was s'posed to be for Virginia. That's what the admiral put about, anyway."

"Yes, I heard tell there was a boat."

"Admiral Winters told me nothing until ready to leave, but then woke me in the middle of the night and brought me with him. He said he couldn't bear to see me swatting flies any longer."

I smiled. Pain shot down my cheek to my chin and I felt my lip split. "Real or imaginary ones?"

"Both. I wanted to tell you as we went, but he wouldn't let me. He said it would give us away and we'd have people moaning and muttering, trying to keep us there. So I left the glove as a clue. Now tell me your story, Master Robin."

"I came to find you, of course. I brought the final emblem."

"Where is it? Let me see."

"I can't. I lost it to the sea, together with my last bit of warm clothing," I confessed. "But Fence, I brought it in my head. The emblem with the big stand of trees. I have solved and memorized it."

"What is it?"

"True it is that it will amaze you," I said.

"Tell me, o tell me," he begged.

"Of course." But when I came to repeat the cipher to him, it was like the turtle eggs, runny and slimy and leaking out of my brain in all directions. In my mind I saw an A, I saw a Y. I saw half of what looked like an O, maybe a backwards C. I could see nothing else and groaned. "God damned stupid message! I can't remember it. Not a single word. It's been knocked out of my head by Proule." This wasn't the first time I'd lost something in the cipher line of business that was important. Memory is a slippery thing. You think you have it by the tail but it can wriggle free and jump out of your net in a flash.

Peter Fence seemed as downcast as I was, but didn't blame me for a moment. "There's a misfortune, but perhaps in time," he said sadly, "you'll remember." He started to suck his thumb. I was used to it now. He always sucked the tip of it when he was upset.

"Perchance I shall. I think I remembered it once before. But now it seems to have vanished from my bonce." My head began to pound again. "I must sleep." I lay down on my good, or at least better, side, pulling my knees up for comfort. Tempest rushed in and lay beside me, his tail thumping against my back. I didn't have the strength to push him away, though true it is, there wasn't even enough room for Fence and myself.

Fence sat for a moment, as I began to drift off. "Before you sleep," he said shyly, taking his thumb from his mouth so he could speak clearly, "I have something to tell you. And this is right good news."

"What is it?"

"Remember what the other emblem said? About the crown and the path?"

"I do."

"Well, listen." He took a deep breath. "I know we searched and searched. But we were searching on the wrong island."

"We were?" I sat back up. My head was still throbbing, but with excitement rather than pain.

"Aye," he said, his eyes bright with pride. "I found a definite path while out gathering wood for the admiral. It's not on the other island. It's here."

"I wonder where it leads to," said I. "I can't wait to find out."

Chapter 23

The Path and a Bath

The next day we were running through the trees to where Fence had found the path. Or at least, he was running. I was limping and hopping as fast as I could. Limp, limp, hop. Limp, limp, hop. And the occasional bump. My head swam, my back burned, as if someone had shoved a hot poker against it, and my heart beat out of time. I should have lain in the lean-to for at least a few more days, thinking of buttery pancakes, of apple pies and raisins, the like of which I'd stolen off barrow boys' stalls back in Plymouth. Those Plymouth Barrows had been my first real treasure trove. But I wanted — no, needed — to see the path for myself, so we could mayhap find an even better treasure. We were getting closer to the secret of the cipher. I could almost smell it. I could also smell my own stink and promised Fence I would take a bath as soon as we were done.

"We call this Winters Island, after the admiral. But to be sure it's part of the Isle of Devils too," said Fence. He picked up some pignuts and threw them in the pail we'd brought with us. Collecting food for the newly-caught swine was what we were supposed to be doing. It was our excuse for being where we were and doing what we were really doing — exploring.

"Yes, the Isle of Devils seems more like a bunch of islands." I gathered some nuts and threw them in the pail.

"Aye. We could call the other Boors Isle. And the admiral says there are even more."

"We saw some of them at least as the *Valentine* foundered. What's at the end of the pathway, Fence?"

"I don't rightly know, Robin. I never dared tread it on my own. I was afraid of what I might find. Witchcraft mayhap. Ghosts. Wild beasts."

He had barely finished talking when I heard twigs snapping. I jumped. But this was no wild beast. It was Mary. She had leapt in front of us and was standing in our way, legs planted like tree trunks, hands on hips. Her tattered skirt trailed down where it had ripped. She shook her fist at me, and I fell back, deathly afraid that another good clip in the head would reopen my half-healed gash.

"I saw your red hair. Bright as flame it is. Brighter 'an my skirt. What you up to? You ain't s'posed to be here, toad spawn. And company," she added nastily, noticing Fence for the first time. "The pair of you should be back at camp labouring, and not leaving all the hard work to others."

"Then why aren't *you* back at the camp, Fish-Finney?" I couldn't stop myself asking.

She advanced towards me, teeth bared, fist up and dangerous. "Who are you to be telling others what to do?"

"You should be asking that question of yourself." I had forgotten my scalp wound. My mouth, as usual, outstripped my sense.

Fence rushed between us before she could get to me. "We are gathering nuts for the pigs, Mistress. The admiral sent us hither to collect food for them as they're no longer free to root for it themselves."

"You ain't telling the truth. You're as bad as toad spawn there."

She now lunged towards Fence, but the pail, thanks be, came to his rescue. He pushed it between them and waved it at her till the the contents rattled. "Don't hit me, Mistress Finney. I'm not lying. Pignuts, these are. Mast, they call them. Nuts for the pigs. I already have a goodly number."

She stopped, glaring but undecided.

"See for yourself." He thrust the pail at her.

"Well," she said, hardly deigning to glance into the pail and clearly disappointed at being cheated out of a fight, "Make sure you fill that bucket, or I'll fetch the admiral down on you."

If anything was an empty threat, this was, and she knew it. With a last backward sneer — "Those ain't real pignuts anyhow. Acorns are real pignuts" — she slunk back into the greenery. I saw a soft ripple in the shadows. It was one of the mariners. He accompanied her. No wonder she wasn't laboring. Not in the usual way, that is. But I didn't care what she did. I was no longer interested in her doings.

"Thank you Fence," I said. "You bested her."

"Lucky we brought the bucket," said the boy, who still looked a bit greenish, as if he would mayhap throw up into it.

"Mary has other fish to fry," I comforted him. "As always. And she's like Tempest, worse bark than bite."

"Tempest has quite a bad bite when roused. Remember him hanging onto that pig? And I wager she does too."

But she had vanished and we continued through the woods. The shadows cast by the tangled boughs grew long and sinister as we went deeper. I took care not to trip over tree roots that crept along the ground. They looked like long gnarled fingers. I wondered that Fence had ever ventured this far by himself.

"I got lost in the forest, and ended up going further while trying to get out," he admitted. "But it turned out to be a lucky mistake. Here we are at the starting point. I think we already passed it twice."

Hell's Bells. Before us was the beginning of the path, narrower than I expected, winding through the trees like a long snake. It was empty of forest leaves, ferns, and bushes. *Someone* had spread pink sand upon it, and *someone* had stuck small pink stones into the ground all the way along its meanders as markers. They glimmered as if to say, "This is the way." I gasped. This path did not make itself, and it wasn't made by animals. Winters Island had at least one other mortal man upon it, or mortal woman, who hadn't come into the Bermudas on the *Valentine*. A person who was there before. Thrilled, I said as much to Fence.

He trembled. "Methinks there is someone in front of us, as you say, someone that we've never met. And there is mayhap someone behind us also, someone we do know. Not Mary. Someone worse." He couldn't bring himself to mention Proule's name, although it was easy enough to work out who he meant. "We are wedged between the unknown and the known."

"Between Scylla and Charybdis?" I asked.

"I don't rightly know who they are."

"Two nasty rock monsters where ships wrecked. If one did not get them, then the other did."

"Aye, like them." He turned around fearfully, as if listening for footsteps, and I turned too, half expecting to see Proule.

We were, true it is, easy enough to dispose of if anyone took a fancy to that line of work. We were like a slab of cheese thrust between two heels of moldy bread. Sooner or later we'd get eaten — like the mariners who tried to scape Scylla — or at best, beaten. All I could see, however, was trees, and all I could hear was leafy whispers. Nothing moved. No one spoke. The place appeared deserted. It was empty of people, save for ourselves. Mary and her friendly sailor were long gone, attending to other business, and I was pretty sure Proule hadn't followed us. I began to feel bolder, more daring. Without a moment of introduction, the old wickedness coursed through my veins.

"We are deep in the forest. No one is here except us. And perhaps a bear or two," I couldn't resist adding.

Fence made a faint sound like a mouse squeak.

"I was jesting, Fence, playing the buffoon. Who knows what we may discover? But not bears, for sure. There are none on either Winters or Boors Island, I'm certain of it, or we would have seen them long ago. Let's go on."

He nodded slowly, his dark hair falling across his face so his blue eyes were hidden. The day was waxing hot, even in the shade. The beginning of the path was lit by a shaft of golden sun. We stood in the centre of the light for the merest trace of time. Then we began to tread the dark forest with its huge boughs and branches that bent towards us. Fence, who hadn't wanted to start, now couldn't wait to finish. "Hurry up, Robin, hurry up. This is taking so long. I have to get there — wherever there is — and back before sundown, or the admiral will be worried."

We followed the ribbon of pink sand down into a valley, around a tall straight tree and southward. At times I could hear the lapping of the waves, and guessed we were near the sea, though I never could see it. As the path was trodden, and the forest grew denser, we grew more excited, and my word pudding began slowly, slowly, to resolve itself back into an emblem cipher. I repeated and repeated it, so I would not forget this time. I didn't tell Fence yet. I was awaiting the proper moment, the moment when we came to the end of the path. I would declaim the next clues in our search proudly. But the path stopped suddenly in a clearing just before a dense copse, and the landscape was immediately discouraging. There was no crown and nothing else that looked even faintly mysterious. Just trees and more trees.

"Fence," I uttered at last, after having looked around, "This is very disheartening. I'd hoped we would find something more. Before us are palms, cedars, and the like, so thickly arrayed that it is almost impossible to traverse them. But there is no crown, as the first cipher promised. On the other hand, I have remembered something else. And my memory agrees with what stands before us."

"Remembered what, Robin?" Fence was sitting on the ground rubbing his foot, the pail, half full of pignuts, beside him. He seemed exhausted and uncaring. "I have a blister," he complained.

I ignored his discomfort, which was certainly no worse than my own, and carried on. "The emblem. That's what I have remembered. I can almost see it in the air in front of me. You must remember it too, from the chest. A thicket, with moon and stars above."

"I do, right well, now that you describe it." He stopped rubbing his foot.

"And here we are, close to a huge tangle of trees, darker and thicker than what we've come through so far. I even remember part of the emblem's verse:

> A Shady wood, portraited to the sight
> With uncouth paths and hidden ways unknown
> Resembling chaos, or the hideous night
> Or those sad groves by banks Bermudian
> With baneful palm and cedar overgrown
> Whose thickest boughs and inmost entries are
> Unpierceable by powers from afar....

"What does 'portraited' mean, Robin? I don't know."

"I don't know either. 'Pictured,' mayhap?" Yes, that had to be right. The emblem was like a picture of the place we were at.

"Aye. I wonder who the powers from afar could be?"

"I'm not sure, perchance Boors and Winters. Certainly not us. We have no power at all, pity 'tis, 'tis true. I've forgotten the rest of the verse, but my brain has mostly unfuddled itself and I do remember the cipher I made from the words: "Through the labyrinth to the cave." I scratched the cipher text in the pink sand at the end of the path with a stick, in case my mind misplaced it again, and I kept staring at it. But it yielded no further secrets. Looking again at the scene before us, I was flummoxed. "Misfortunately I see neither maze nor cave."

"I know why! I know why!" Fence had leapt to his feet and was dancing around.

Unable to dance myself, I instead bestowed on him a questioning gaze.

"Because it's light and not dark. We have to come back by moon and starlight, so it looks like the emblem."

And that's exactly why Fence, untutored though he might be, was my good and clever boy. "Yes, of course you're right. We'll wait here. Come nightfall, perhaps grave secrets will be unlocked. We will pierce the inmost entries of the grove before us." I sounded very pompous, even to myself. But the emblem seemed to demand flowery language.

"Not tonight, Robin. The sun is well past the midpoint, and I have to get this food back for the swine. And whatever else we can carry. Some of those little prune things, mayhap. Tree berries. So no one will notice aught amiss."

I was fed up. We had come so far and were perchance so close that I was desperate to go on. I could hardly bear to hobble all the way back to our smelly lean-to full of dog and then come forth again. I said as much.

"I'm sorry, but we shall do better anyways in two nights' time when the moon is full and the night is bright with stars, Robin, shan't we?"

"I am determined to go on, even by myself. You go back if you have to."

"I see the clouds beginning to roll in." Fence sounded desperate. "And I thought I felt a drop of rain just then. The wind is beginning to blow. Tonight won't be the right night for finding out. And I must not disappoint the pigs or the admiral won't let me out again."

Mayhap this had nothing to do with getting back to feed the pigs. Mayhap he was just too frighted to continue, but in any case, I was too tired to argue with him. It would be a long and painful argument. He usually deferred to me, but now his lips were set in a determined line; however, not arguing was not the same as accepting. "You go back if you must," I said again. "I will go on by myself, having come this far."

"What shall I say to the admiral if he asks where you are?"

I shrugged. "Hell's Bells, Fence, I don't give a twig what you tell him. Tell him you lost me."

"You're not well enough to go forward on your own."

"I am not sick enough to go *back*. I will go forward if I can find a way. Do what you want. You needn't worry about me." I didn't want my words to sound harsh and bitter, but they did. They stung him, I could see, but I did nothing to heal his hurt.

"Very well then." Fence picked a handful of small berry-like fruits. Chewing one and throwing the rest into the pail, he began to walk slowly back along the path. He turned his head to glance at me twice, but did not return. As soon as he'd gone, I felt my meanness in my bones, and was sorry for it. How stupid I was! I'd come to Winters Island to find my only friend, yet here I was without him. And all because I was too impatient to wait two days. He had lived through enough unkindness. He didn't need more. The memory of the long S on his hand haunted me.

I erased the sand cipher with my foot. I felt foolish and lonely, and would even have welcomed the company of the damned dog. But I would strip off and bathe in the sea, which must be close by as I could hear it still. Not deep would I go, though. The sea was too treacherous, and I had already learned all the evil lessons it cared to teach. I would wash my clothes in the waves and put them back on, wet and stiff with salt though they might be. At the moment they stank as badly as I did, and I wished to go into the future clean, not surrounded by my own stench. Finally I would sit down to wait for the sun to fall behind the clouds and into the depths of the ocean. I was greatly afeard, and wanted my good friend Fence. But I wanted even more to see what night would reveal.

The sun went down, the moon came up. It was orange, huge, and almost round, near the horizon. It had just a small section bitten off the edge. Moon mice, I thought. I couldn't see any stars, and true it is, soon the moon itself, as it rose, was partly hidden by cloud, through which it glimmered, revealing a message carved into a tree trunk:

> As you journey through this wood
> Rest when needed, as you should.
> Take the mazed path for a while
> Hasten from the villains vile.
> Unless you visit you'll be found,
> Roughly treated, brought to ground.
>
> Don't stop here but come inside.
> Underground you must abide.
> Doubt not you will solve the clue,
> Labyrinth will guide you through.
> End your journey at the cave,
> You will find the wealth you crave.

Someone is here besides me, I thought. Someone who knows who I am and what I'm doing. But who were the villains? Proule and Mary? Or someone else? And how would they bring us to ground? There was word of the labyrinth again in the message, and the cave. It was exciting and frightening together. I shivered. The moon was now totally obscured, and it was black as a graveyard at midnight. Perchance corpses would rise up and dance. I could almost feel their feathery fingers. I looked to the stand of trees, or at least, towards where I believed them to be. I could see nothing at first, but soon they, or rather a host of spiders' webs hanging from them, began to glow eerily, a green gleaming against the darkness. And I could hear a constant low chattering, which scared me stupid, cowardly, whey-faced moldwarp that I am.

Nevertheless, I went closer. I couldn't resist. The webs grew brighter. The spiders in their centres were big as plates, winking gold and silver and pearl, like jewelled escutcheons. These were the chatterers. They made the noise by rubbing their legs together, though I had never heard spiders make any kind of sound before. The bright webs were surrounding what I could now see to be a dark circular area. It looked like an entrance, although a very strange and sinister one. I blinked twice, but the round opening — if opening it was — remained. It must be the beginning of the labyrinth.

I suddenly remembered both the Latin inscription on our first cipher and what it meant: *Mente Videbor* — "By the mind I shall be seen." Somehow I was seeing the opening to the labyrinth with my mind rather than with my eyes. But before I had a chance to go through it, or even contemplate doing so, I glimpsed a weird and terrifying flickering. An old man I'd never seen before was standing very close to me, close enough to touch, light reflecting onto him from the webs and streaming away in all directions.

I was too amazed to move. Indeed, my legs had turned to jelly, so I couldn't go anywhere. There was a distant grumbling of thunder. It sounded like a belly that needed food.

"Come with me," the old man said, his voice raspy as a rusty key in a lock, "I will lead you through." Just then a brilliant shaft of lightning, forking down from the heavens, struck the ground around him. It was followed immediately by a deafening thunderstroke. Rain began to pour down in torrents. The man spoke again, but I could not hear what he said. Nor did I want to. He might be one of the villains. Terrified, I turned and fled.

Chapter 24

Raising a Storm

The storm was dreadful, as bad as anything on the *Valentine*, and for all I knew the rusty-voiced old man might have come after me. I had no idea whether he meant me good or evil, nor did I care to hang around and find out. I went as fast as I could, running, limping, banging into cedars, tripping over bushes, over the long fronds of ferns, and making my injuries worse. Occasionally lightning illumined the path and I could see my way better for a moment, but I was soon pitched into darkness again as the thunder crashed, the waves nearby roared, and the rain beat down.

"No one in their right mind would be out in this," I comforted myself. "Except me. So the old man won't be either." But I couldn't convince myself. Perchance he was a wizard who had caused the thunderstorm himself. He certainly looked like one with his long hair, white beard, and loose robe. He might catch and imprison me in the message tree, or do worse, and no one would ever see me again. I wished a hundred times that I'd listened to Fence.

Finally, after what seemed like hours of limping and worrying, I reached our lean-to, gasping for air. I was scratched and sore and wet through, but more than relieved to be back with no one behind me. I dived headlong into our shelter, falling on top of both Fence and Tempest in my haste. True it is, it was a very small, stinky space.

Tempest yelped. I yelped back.

"Get off. You're soaked. I warned you it was going to rain," said Fence nastily. He gave me a shove. "And I told the admiral you were lost, as you said I should. But it's too late to tell him you're found, though now, at least, I can sleep without worrying."

"Don't sleep yet," I said, rubbing a particularly damp and painful part of myself. "I was wet even before the storm hit. Not that that matters. But I have so much to say to you."

"In the morning. Not before." He yawned and was asleep in a minute, his nose making a faint bubbly sound as he breathed. Tempest was soon snoring too. He was lying on his back with his paws in the air, silly beast that he was. I pushed him into Fence, squelched down in as small a space as possible so as not to lie on his tail, and shivered.

Chapter 25

Early Rising

I couldn't wait to tell Fence, but come morning there was much else to think about. The rain had stopped, and it was already waxing hot. I crawled forward and poked my head out to get the moldy stink of damp clothing and dog out of my nostrils. But there, right in front of me, stood Proule, a vicious expression on his face. I tried to duck my head back in, but he'd already seen me, and pulled on my hair to prevent me from disappearing. He placed his boot on my hand.

"Here yer are, cockroach, and God blind me if I ain't been searching for yer all the livelong night." He let go of my hair and stood straight. But he kept his foot on my hand and pressed.

"I'm very sorry, Master Proule, but I found my way home very late indeed, after bumping into a great number of trees," I said apologetically, staring up at him from my lowly position. I had learned to be very, very polite to Proule, and didn't mean to change my usual behaviour while he was treading on my fingers.

"Winters sent me and some others out after yer, damn him. Like I ain't needing my sleep. That man has ideas above his station."

"Well, thank you for looking." As it happened, I was very glad he hadn't found me, or I might not be here now, very uncomfortably half in and half out of the lean-to. I felt at rather a disadvantage, with him standing there so tall and sweaty, and me trapped on my hands and knees, unable to either go all the way out or all the way back in.

"I'll be watching yer, cockroach. Don't disappear again. I want yer where I can see yer." He took his boot off my fingers and placed it on my neck.

"No, sir. Yes, sir," I muttered, unable to move.

There was a long pause. Finally, he removed his foot. "Get along with yer," he hissed, and I took this as a cue to withdraw my hand and duck my head back into the lean-to.

After a few minutes I poked it out again, just to make sure he'd gone. He had. Or at least, he wasn't within punching or kicking or smelling distance. I was beginning to understand better why tortoises vanished into their shells. True it is, I was feeling a bit like one myself, my head coming and going as it did. I wondered if tortoises ever got dizzy.

Chapter 26

A Stolen Hoard

Fence and I were standing a little way off from the camp, hidden by trees. I was explaining what I'd seen the night before in the way of verses, cobwebs, old men, and lightning, trembling at the memory of it all, when we heard a clamour nearby.

It was Proule and Mary Finney. "You stole my shillings," she screamed. "All I had in the world for my old age." She clutched his shoulder and began to drag him towards camp.

Proule tried to disengage himself. He couldn't get her hand off him so he punched her twice in the belly. She doubled over.

"Listen good, or yer won't *make* it to old age. I ain't even seen yer stupid shillings, woman. And how did *yer* come by them? Huh?"

"You have 'em, I know it," she gasped. "Buyers said he won two shillings off you last night, and you're usually skint."

"He's a liar. Those shillings I give him are mine and always were," Proule yelled. "Now shut yer yap or I'll give yer a hiding so bad yer'll crawl into a hole and croak there." He hit her again, and she crumpled. Certainly Proule seemed in a terrible mood this day, mayhap from lack of sleep. But that was no reason to hit a woman, even a poor excuse for one like Mary Finney. Besides, she was the only woman we had on the island, and she did the cooking. Fence ran to her, and after a moment's hesitation I followed.

"Go away, Master Proule, you bad, evil man," yelled Fence, shaking his fist and displaying his reckless — and to my mind rather stupid — courage.

"Why, yer...."

"Go away or I'll tell the admiral," Fence shouted, waving his arms at Proule and then throwing them around Mary, who was still winded.

"And I'll see that he does," mumbled I at last, finding my tongue. I hated Mary, but I hated Proule more. And I had to support Fence, who had supported me often enough. If that meant I might possibly worm my way into Mary's graces, so much the better. I had enemies enough and to spare. And I couldn't help but remember the tall tree's message.

Tempest rushed out of nowhere, as dogs are apt to do, on his way to somewhere else. And he bit Proule on the knee. This was no doubt at least in part revenge for past crimes.

"Hear, hear, what's going on?" cried Beerson, running up to us.

"Nothing. There ain't nothing going on," yelled Proule, swatting at Tempest. "That blinking cur bit the hell out of my knee."

"Hear, hear," Beerson said again, kicking the dog as he clearly didn't know which of the two, man or beast, was the miscreant.

Tempest removed his canines from Proule's flesh and growled mightily at Beerson. But he knew when he was outnumbered. He left fast, tail between his legs.

"He stole my shillings," groaned Mary, "the dung-faced thief. They were in the pouch attached to my skirt. I've carried some of them all the way here from England and earned the others on the voyage. Rightly earned by an honest woman, washing clothes and cooking for the crew. For my old age, y'know. Now they're gone and the pouch is gone too."

"There, there, mistress. We'll track the mongrel down and recover the pouch. Mayhap it's in its mouth."

"I ain't talking about the the dog, you dimwit. I'm talking about Proule."

"Sorry mistress." Beerson looked around for the culprit but the culprit had vanished.

"He stole my money *and* he socked me in the belly. Not once but thrice. These boys, though it pains me to say it, ain't involved." She paused before adding grudgingly, "They likely saved me from a worse roughing up."

"Don't you worry. I shall tell the admiral," said Beerson. "He'll get to the bottom of it one way or another, praise the Lord."

As Beerson helped Mary back to camp, with us following, she turned to me. "I've misjudged you, Starveling, and though I ain't exackly sorry for it, as you're such a rude little parasite, I'll be sure to try an' treat you better in future."

As this seemed both a compliment and an insult bound up together, I just nodded, not sure how to reply.

We were soon at Winters' hut.

"We have no dungeon here. Take two crewmen and fetch Proule. Tie him to a tree so he cannot escape," Winters ordered Beerson, when he heard. "Let me think on this matter further, for he has performed other outrages lately. I will hear evidence, and we shall have a proper trial."

"When shall we have it, sir?" asked Beerson.

"In three days, to give us time to prepare."

"That means we can still go to the maze tomorrow night, at the time of the full moon," Fence whispered to me.

"Huh? I'm not so sure that's a good idea." The very thought of the labyrinth now filled me with dismay.

Winters was still talking: "That is my ruling, Beerson. Find Proule immediately, and keep him safely bound until Friday." I was suddenly glad to be here on this island with the admiral, and not back on the other one with that lunatic Boors, who would certainly forget who Proule was less than a half hour into the trial, if not before.

"Proule can't hurt you now," Fence said, after they had caught him. We were friends again and I grinned at him. Later I silently ticked off a list of the villains who according to the message tree might run me to ground. There were none left! Scratcher was stuck on the other island; Mary was reformed; and Proule was securely tied to the trunk of a tall palm tree.

If my head hadn't still pounded and thumped every now and then, I would have cantered for joy. Later I realized that who was absent could in certain circumstances become present, and that who was tied could come untied. I shivered at the thought. Also, those who were reformed could fall back into their old ways, but somehow I didn't believe that would happen with Mary. She knew where her bread was buttered, as I had said once or twice of myself. As Scratcher had said of me. Not that there was any butter here. Nor bread neither.

Chapter 27

Small Beer and Mince Pies

I hadn't wanted to retrace my steps along the path. But the most interesting thing about my friendship with Fence was that when one of us wanted to back out of an adventure, the other was usually hot to be on its trail. I had been full of excitement and vigor two days before, when Fence had trotted away with his pail bumping against his knee. Now it was his turn to urge me on, as we sat in the lean-to. "Just think, Robin, we have come this far. We've solved the verses and ciphers — at least for the most part. You've found the entrance to the labyrinth itself. Not much left. Only the cave and the crown to discover. The royal treasure itself. We can't play the weasel now."

"Play the weasel?"

"Give up."

"You're very brave all of a sudden," I said sourly.

"I had a think that time you went on by yourself, and I realized it was right cowardly of me to go back."

"I don't blame you for that. True it is, I should have returned with you. But I didn't. Still, things being as they are, you don't know what frighted me. You haven't seen the old wizardy man with the white beard. You haven't seen the many-branched lightning or heard the thunder crash like cymbals. You haven't seen the message tree or branches alight with glittering cobwebs or the spiders blazing within or … uh…." I ran out of breath and words at the same time.

"You described them to me right well, as you're now doing all over again. And remember, we defeated Proule, who's a real devil. The men caught and bound him. I reckon we could stand against anyone or anything, as long as we stick together. And mayhap we could take Tempest with us. He can be brave as a lion too."

Tempest yawned.

"Besides," continued Fence, "we don't even know if the old man you spoke of is evil."

"True." But I still hadn't wanted to go.

That night, though, Peter Fence woke me from a dream of mince pies and small beer, which I'd stolen off the barrows often enough in the past. Bleary with sleep, but with wickedness rising somewhat fitfully within me, as well as a sense of loyalty to Fence, I agreed we should find the labyrinth again. This time, perchance, we would journey through it to the bright or bitter end.

Chapter 28

Underneath the Trees

We were at the end of the pathway, having turned around and doubled back several times to ensure no one was following us. The dog appeared and disappeared, appeared and disapeared again, in and around trees and shrubs and tall feathery ferns. At one point he must have gone for a swim, because he came back soaked and shook himself all over us. Phew. There is nothing quite like the smell of wet dog, unless it's dead dog. My nose wrinkled in disgust.

It was now about midnight, the full moon shining hard upon the path, turning its sand grains into tiny gems. The stars, too, winked like diamonds. There were hundreds upon hundreds of them. It was almost as bright as daylight. The scene before us was an exact reflection of the cipher, except spider webs shone golden green, showing the way into the labyrinth. No thunder, no lightning, not a single message on a single tree, and not a cloud in the sky. The old man hadn't shown his face either this night. I took a deep breath. Suddenly, the second verse of the emblem, which I'd thought lost forever, came back to me, and I recited it to Fence:

> Here is the picture that I did devise
> To show thee simply how men should not be:
> An inward wood, unsearched with outward
> eyes
> A thousand angles light will never see.
> But thou who art of open heart and free,
> True as thou dost pass along the way,
> Shalt know what's to be known and not
> betray.

"What can it mean, Robin?"

"I think it means that we two will be safe in the labyrinth, as we're both of open heart, and you at least are honest."

"You are, too."

I would have laughed aloud had I not been so afeard. "Oh, Fence, if you only knew the sum of my wickedness."

"If it's in the past, I don't need to know. And it's better that I don't." Fence took a deep breath before stepping off the path and onto the grass. I joined him, and we moved cautiously into the stand of trees. At the entrance the spiders winked at us, their webs like giant fishing nets, seeming to draw us in. They shone emerald and gold. The moon shone silver. But once inside, the webs disappeared, the moon and stars went out like candles, and there was no light at all. I had spots before my eyes in the velvet dark. And there was neither the sound of the sea nor any other noise save that of my own heart, beating loud and fast.

Tempest lunged at me and began to bark. "Sh," I whispered. "You'll wake the wizard." He took no notice. I grabbed the fur on his back and told Fence to do likewise. "Dogs can see at night. He'll lead us through."

"Aye," agreed Fence. After Tempest had bumped us into several large obstacles, however, I remembered that it was cats that could see in the dark and let him go.

But as my eyes became accustomed to the dark, I began to see grey and foggy outlines of trees and bushes, and a confusing profusion of paths. We started along one, only to have it stop a few yards in. We retraced our steps and started on another, only to have it crisscross many others and lead us back to what appeared to be the beginning. "This is like my life," I groaned after several more tries, "lots of wrong turnings."

"But it certainly is a labyrinth, so we're on the way to where we should be. The cave, remember?"

"How could I forget?" I snapped, beginning to feel very tired indeed. I wished I was back at camp and asleep in the lean-to.

"We shouldn't give up, Robin. The next path might be the one. And at least Tempest has stopped barking."

In fact the dog had disappeared altogether. Soon he came bounding back. He grabbed Fence by the shirt and pulled.

"He knows the way! He knows the way!" Fence, triumphant, allowed himself to be dragged along. I followed, of course. But true it is, Tempest didn't know the way, not through the labyrinth, at least. What he did know was the way to the nearest coney warren, a maze in miniature, you might say. When we reached the hole that led into it, he stopped dead He was barking madly again and I could hear him digging with his paws.

I sighed and cast my eyes down despairingly. Then I realized: there was something quite different about this path. Beginning at the warren, it was studded with fan-shaped cockle shells, which glowed in the awful dark. "Look, Fence, look here. Someone has done this on purpose to guide us. This must be the way."

"You mean all we have to do is follow the shells?"

"Yes, along ways both curved and straight. Now see if you can get that dog to stop his racket." I tried to hide the fact that I was almost pissing myself with excitement.

"Aye, I'll pinch his nose, see if that'll do it."

It didn't.

We left Tempest barking and followed the cockle shell path. It meandered mysteriously through darkness, the sharp branches of trees and needles of bushes scratching us as we went. I heard frogs and night insects, whereas before it had been silent, save for the dog's racket. Once I thought I heard a shrill and hollow laugh. Fence must have heard it too, because he suddenly clung to me. But whether it really was a laugh, or a shrieking nightbird, or even a creaking bough, we knew not. And it was not repeated.

At last the path stopped. The clearing in front of it signalled the end of the labyrinth, and we emerged slowly, our eyes blinking in the light. True it is, the moon and stars were brilliant again in the night sky. It was as if they'd been waiting for us, and were shining all the harder for seeing us safe. I looked around. We were very close to the shore, and likely on the other side of the island from our camp. I wasn't very good at reading the sky and position of the stars, so I couldn't be certain. But, "We're on the far southwest side of Winters Island," said Fence, whose natural knowledge often proved very useful.

The sea roared. I could see by the expanses of wet and muddy sand that the tide was receding. Each time a wave broke on the shore, it was a little further out. There was not a single footprint, apart from our own, anywhere on the wet sand, nor the dry sand neither. Not even a pawprint. I felt we had reached the end of the world. If there were other islands further west or south of us, we couldn't see them. The ocean seemed to stretch forever. The dog had stayed behind to worry the conies, his yapping growing ever softer as we drew further and further away from him. Distance had finally muted him. I imagined he was still at the warren, having totally forgotten us.

"I still don't see a crown," said Fence, as if expecting one to pop up on the grass. "If there's a cave, it will be over yonder." Fence pointed to a tumble of high rocks beyond the sand dunes and tall grasses that lined the shore. "Let's hurry. There's a red glow in the sky."

"It can't be long till daybreak. And we still have to find our way back." I scrambled over the dunes and up the rocks with him, my feet slipping and sliding. Trees grew on the rocks, their long and twisting roots tangling with one another and trailing down towards the sand. I had never seen anything like them before, but I'd never have managed to climb to the top without them. I grasped a thin trunk here or a stringy root there to stop myself from crashing down.

It was hard finding anything in the muddled tangle of rocks and trees, but of course that's the way it should be. We were, after all, at what I judged to be the end of a long trail of emblems, clues, pathways, and mazes. How could we expect finding the cave to be anything but difficult? "It's like climbing the rigging in the *Valentine*," said Fence, completely out of breath, and sliding back a little every time he moved forward.

But what was that ahead? A hole — a rather large one. Jagged rocks lined it, like the teeth of a huge and fearsome beast. "I think we've just reached the crow's nest," I announced. "Or at least, what we're searching for.... There's what looks to be an entrance right here, right at the top, among the highest rocks and trees. Looks dangerous, like a corcodillo with its mouth wide open."

"Aye, you're right."

We both peered in, taking care not to snag ourselves on the sharp-toothed rocks. The hole smelled of dank and cold, a strange odour that I'd only smelled once or twice before — in English caves where I'd hidden when I had nowhere safe to be. "It's very dim. What do you see, Fence?"

"Not much at all, Robin ... I wish we'd had a candle to bring, though it would have burnt out by now. It's very dark, except ..." he paused and craned his neck, "there looks to be a passageway, slanting down. But I can't be sure."

"There's only one way to find out." My heart racing, I began to clamber in. I scratched an arm as I went, but it bled little. "Well, what are you waiting for, Fence?"

"The old man. I'm greatly afeard he's down there." Fence was shaking, and a tear, which I pretended not to notice, squeezed out of the corner of his eye.

"Me too, but just think: The dog made enough racket to wake the dead, yet we didn't see hide nor hair of the man. And his footprints aren't in the sand below. Perhaps I was mistaken altogether, and only *imagined* I saw him. I did still have a pretty bad bump on the head, true it is. But even if he is down there, we'll deal with it somehow. As you said yourself, we've stood against Proule. And we've already done the hard work and found almost all there is to find."

"I did say those things, didn't I? At the moment I wish to Heaven I hadn't." But Fence, after a sad groan, climbed in, very, very carefully, and on we went, past long thin outcrops descending from the ceiling like stone swords. It grew no darker, but it grew no lighter either. There was only distance and freezing cold, more distance and more cold. Down, down, down we went, hellwards, through many winding passages. Sometimes we slipped. Sometimes we skidded. Once, Fence's big head banged hard into a stone sword. I had managed to avoid it, but turning when he cried "Ouch," I tripped over another growing upwards from the floor. Eventually, there was sharp pain between and behind my eyes from the cold, and I could barely breathe. But the passage widened suddenly, and we found ourselves in a large and somewhat smoky cave, lit by torches.

"Hell's Bells," I muttered, staggered by the size of it, and the fact that it was furnished, although somewhat oddly.

"Someone lives here, Robin," whispered Fence. "It looks like a chamber. There's a fire, and a chair, and a bed."

This was indeed so, but both the chair and the bed were of stone, although hung with palm leaves. They seemed to be natural outcrops of the cave. The fireplace, built in a circle of small nuggets of rock, sat directly below a narrow hole in the ceiling of the cave that must have stretched all the way to outside, or the inside would be full of smoke, the air unbreathable. The fire in the grate burned bright red and yellow, with wisps of blue flame flying up through crackling logs.

Misfortunately, there was not a jot of treasure that I could see. No crown neither. But the cave was decorated with cedar branches and purple berries, both on the floor and along the walls. It all looked rather merry, like Yuletide. An old song that I'd learned years before knocked on my bonce, demanding admittance. Something mad had got into me, mayhap the happy realization that though the wished for treasure was nowhere about, neither was the old man. I began to hop and dance around the fire singing:

> Be merry, be merry,
> My friend withal,
> For friends should be treasured,
> Both short and tall;
> Tis merry in hall, when tongues wag all,
> And welcome Merry Yuletide.

"Shh, Robin, someone might hear you." From the way Fence said "someone," I knew exactly who he meant. "And it's not Christmas anyway. It's too late in the year, between Yuletide and Shrovetide. Besides, there are no presents," he finished lamely, warming his hands by the fire.

The S on the back of his right hand stood out in stark relief against the flames. My merriness vanished. I stopped myself from stating the obvious: That there were never any presents for such as us, foundlings that we were. Not at Christmas, nor at Shrove or New Year, nor any other time. Not so much as a crumb from a plum pudding. For a moment I felt really sorry for myself, and for Fence too. But I was distracted by a glimpse of something hanging off the back of the chair. It was half hidden by palm leaves, so I hadn't noticed it before. It shimmered and glowed in the firelight. I blinked and looked again. I couldn't believe my eyes.

"Look at this, Fence," I said, my voice rising with excitement. "I believe we've found what we're looking for. We've found the best Christmas present ever! We've found the Golden Prize!"

Chapter 29

Robin's Find

"Here it is," I said, as I moved to the back of the chair and picked the object up. It was a long and heavy chain, which slipped easily through my fingers. "This is treasure indeed."

Fence clapped his hands and laughed aloud. "I *knew* we should find it. What's that on the chain?" he asked, his cheeks red as apples in the firelight.

"It's a pendant, a medallion, a golden medallion covered in precious gems," said I, examining it. "There is something engraved on it. A strange-looking bird. Come see."

Fence studied it carefully. "It's a bird on a bed of flames, just like the flames of this fire." He turned it over and over again.

"The engraving seems familiar. I'm sure I once knew what the bird represents, but have forgotten. It must be worth a fortune."

"We should put it back now, Robin."

"Don't be daft. We should swipe it, swipe it and run." I grinned. My wickedness was rising fast, with its old whoosh and flash hardly tarnished. "If we ever get back to England, or even to Virginia, we'll be rich as Croesus."

"It isn't ours to take," said Fence flatly.

"We can bolt with it fast. I'm good at that."

"You seem to forget we were led here. The old man wanted us to come or we'd never have found the entrance. He invited you into the labyrinth, you told me so. We're sort of his guests. He put his trust in us. We should leave the necklace where we found it."

"That would mean we'd made so much effort, for such small reward."

"Virtue is its own reward," Fence replied smugly. As if I didn't know he'd been as enthusiastic as I was at the thought of treasure.

"You're not so virtuous. You've lied before, mostly for my sake. What's the difference between lying and thieving?"

"Quite a bit. My lies saved you once or twice, but without really hurting anyone. No one, as I know of, was ever hanged for a fib or two told in service of a friend. Stealing, on the other hand, is a capital offence."

I sniffed. Fence was too perfect for his own good. I could almost see a halo above his head. What had he thought we were going to do with treasure once we found it, if not nick it? What was the point of reading all those emblems, of solving all those ciphers, of risking the wrath of Scratcher, otherwise?

I asked him. His answer was plain enough. "I didn't think it would belong to anyone. This does. It doesn't seem like stealing if it's buried or shipwreck booty, if it once belonged to people who are long gone. They wouldn't miss it. Stealing something owned by a living person is unforgivable, in my book. My own inheritance, the farm and all the sheep, was stole from me by my stepfather. I can never forget it. And not only that," he added. "If we take the necklace, the old man will surely find us. He could be somewhere hidden, watching us this very minute. In fact, this could be a test."

I snorted with derision and we began to argue. We almost came to blows. Fence knocked the medallion out of my hand and onto the floor. I raised a closed fist to punch him, but dropped it instantly. What was I doing, fighting with my only friend? And as it happened, in a certain way Fence was right. This medallion did belong to someone. If we took it now, its owner would almost certainly follow us. It wouldn't be hard for him to catch us, one way or another, and then we'd have a really slippery mess to slide our way out of. This wasn't like grabbing a piece of pie or loaf of bread off the barrows, and that had been reckless enough. This was something worth a king's ransom, and we would almost certainly be hunted down for it.

But I was still fixed on the idea of possessing it. Its brilliant colours glittered behind my eyes when I shut them. It was the closest I'd ever been to riches. There must be a way to nick it and its heavy gold chain without getting my hand chopped off in the process. After all, what did the old man need it for, here on an island, miles from anywhere? I wasn't doing him any real harm. I, on the other hand, planned to return to England. The medallion still lay on the ground. I went down on my knees, as if worshipping it. My fingers crept towards it. I took no responsibility for them. They were acting of their own accord. Soon they caught and clutched it.

"Stop that, Robin," Fence said sternly. "It's staying here."

Hell's Bells. But I swallowed my anger. I might not get it now but I'd figure out a solution and act on it. Next time, if Fence was determined to stay saintly, I'd come alone. I'd leave him polishing his halo.

Rather angrily, I slung the flaming bird and chain back on the chair, where they dangled in all their golden glory. But then, unable to resist, I picked the damn thing up again.

"Robin?"

"What is it now?"

"I can hear heavy, raspy breathing. Not you or me. A wild beast. Or someone *old*."

I dropped the medallion. We turned tail. After we scrambled, or rather tumbled, from the rocks to the shore,

Fence stopped dead. I looked where he was looking and saw something etched deep into the wet sand:

UKQ DWRA YKIA PK REOEP IA
BNKI PDA IAOOWCA K* PDA PNAA
XQP PDKQCD EI BNWEH W*Z KHZ
ZK *KP OPAWH IU CKHZ

"What's that?" Fence yelled. "It looks like a spell."

"Sh," I whispered. "I've no idea. And I'm not stopping to find out. There are large footprints around it. You won't stop either if you want to keep your guts and gizzard intact. Come on."

I gave him a shove to get him started again. He shrieked. We ran for our lives.

Chapter 30

Evil Scratcher

I didn't have time to think further about the strange message on the shore. For as we neared our lean-to, who did I see with his graying hair and evil expression but Scratcher! How did he get across from the other island? And how did he know where to come? Never mind, he was here. Too big to get into our shelter, he was standing on the grass beside it, scratching his ear. He was talking to Trusty and Ruffles, but he was waiting for me. As we came down the hill, he pointed right at me.

"Get over here, you pathetic excuse for an insect, you weaselly worm, you disgusting lump of lard," he yelled, "or I'll come over there and fetch you." He stamped his feet hard and snorted like a stallion. Spittle flew from his lips. I didn't know what he wanted, but I didn't wish to find out, either.

For a few seconds I was frozen to the spot. *Stupid Starveling, too scared to scarper*, taunted a little voice in my ear. So much for that: I wasn't about to be called a coward by anyone, not even myself. Scratcher snorted again. Perchance he was sure I would come to him when called, but I was off and running without more ado. He took off after me, panting hard. My bad leg slowed me up a little, but even so, I was much faster than he was. He hadn't done anything in the way of exercise for months, except lift his beer to his lips or clop me round the noggin. He didn't have an icicle's chance in Hades of catching up with me.

CHAPTER 31

IN THE LABYRINTH

I spent a day and a night in the forest labyrinth, totally miserable and hungry, but confident that Scratcher wouldn't discover me there. He didn't, but Peter Fence, who knew the secret entrance, did. Fence came upon me on the second morning. I had hidden myself under branches, but he called out. Recognizing his voice, I answered immediately.

"Praise be I've found you," he said, handing me a couple of baked eggs he'd carried with him. "I've been tramping all over. The admiral wants you. He needs you to give evidence against Mortimer Proule. You and Mary both."

This scared me even more. "No, Fence, I'd have to be crazy to go back. Another sharp head knock from Scratcher, or anyone else for that matter, and my brains will spill out. I was too afeard even to go on to the cave, in case he caught me on the way."

"Or in case the wizard caught you inside?"

"True it is." I grimaced.

"Scratcher, though, wouldn't be able to find you here in the maze. In any case, Admiral Winters says he'll shelter you from him. He told me to find you and tell you, so there's no need to worry on that account."

"No one can protect me from Scratcher."

"The admiral is stern, but he's a right good man. You can trust him. He's helped you before. And he's been keeping Scratcher beside him in camp while I find you. He knows of Scratcher's cruelty. Besides, you can't stay out much longer. You'll starve, sure as eggs is eggs," he said, as the last one disappeared down my gullet.

"I can wring the necks of birds. I can catch conies and roast 'em on a spit. I can also go down to the shore and fish." But it wasn't an inviting prospect. I couldn't hide *and* fish at the same time, and though I was expert at eating small animals, I wasn't half as adept at catching them. If I was fast, they were faster. And doing the actual killing would make me feel a bit queasy, if the truth be known. I loved the taste of bacon, but was sick to my belly at the smell and the blood when Oldham killed the yearly pig. I didn't want to give in too easily, though. It would look weak as small beer, so it took a bit more persuasion from Fence before I agreed to return.

"Scratcher says that Sir Thomas Boors told him where we were," said Fence as we made our way through the trees.

"Boors must have had a sane moment."

"So Scratcher took the rowboat, and came right over."

"He thinks I'm his by right," I said angrily. "Not a servant but a slave. He thinks if he whistles I'll come running."

"Not anymore," said Fence, "Not after he called you and you ran fast as lightning the other way. But he'll have to take the rowboat back to Boor's island, right enough, and then we'll be rid of him. It's all that the colonists there have to travel the sea."

"That won't make a jot or tittle of difference to Scratcher." I was glum.

"There's something else," said Fence. "The admiral sent me to Proule's hut to see what I could find."

"And?"

"Mary's pouch was stuffed between two cedar boughs he was using for a roof. I looked up and saw the corner of it. There was no mistaking it. It was the same material and the same dirty red as her skirt, No shillings in it though." He drew the pouch from his sleeve, showed it to me, then stuffed it back in.

I whistled. Mary was right all along. Proule had nicked her money. Of course, if I'd have known about it, I might have nicked it first. But I was careful to say nothing of the kind to Fence. There was something about the air on Winters Island. It got into the heart of me and was making me more devious than ever, just when I wanted to be straight.

So, "Have you told Winters what you found?" I asked instead.

"Not yet. I feel right mean to rat on anyone, even Proule. But the admiral sent me on an errand. So I have to report back as soon as we return to camp."

As we left the labyrinth, I had the unsettling feeling that someone was watching us. It wasn't the first time. Not by a long chalk. The night before I'd woken in the middle of the maze with that same prickly feeling. I'd peered through a hole in the branches to see the old man staring down at me, lantern in hand. It was as if I wasn't hidden at all. I'd cried out, greatly afeard, and he had vanished into the gloom.

Chapter 32

No Mercy!

A small crowd had gathered to see Proule lambasted. Many thought it the best entertainment since we'd left England. They were behaving as if they were at the village fair and Proule was one of the freaks. There was much merriment and throwing of eggs at sticks or into buckets. Men sitting on logs were eating tortoise and fowl flesh. A mariner was roasting a pig on a spit, Mary being otherwise occupied during the proceedings. Scratcher, who was standing next to Winters, glowered at me from afar.

"Hear ye, hear ye." Beerson shouted above the noise, looking extremely uncomfortable in his new role. "At the command of Admiral Winters, we are here for the trial of Mortimer Proule, late of the county of Essex in England. God save the King."

"God save the King," one or two people echoed. A couple more clapped.

I thought Beerson had done speaking, but after a short pause he went on: "And suddenly there was with the angel a multitude of the heavenly host praising God, and saying, Glory to God in the highest, and on earth, peace, good will towards men." Having finished this strange and inappropriate speech, he sat down on the crumbling stump of a cedar, clearly relieved that he'd done his duty.

"Fetch the prisoner," instructed Winters.

Proule, who had been tied to a nearby tree, was unbound and brought into a circle marked out with small pieces of pink rock. He smelled worse than ever.

"Mortimer Proule, you stand accused of first, beating the boy Robin Starveling mercilessly, and second, stealing Mary Finney's shillings. How do you plead with regard to beating Robin Starveling?"

"Yer don't have the right to govern me. It's not England or the ship. I'll do what I ruddy well want." Proule spat onto the grass.

"I am the governor of this island, by the grace of God and the King, and permission of Sir Thomas Boors. We will try you whether you will it or no. Do you understand?"

"Aye," Proule answered grudgingly. "But though yer try me, I ain't submitting to yer governance."

"Shame!" a man shouted, and his cry was taken up by others. Someone threw an egg at Proule. It cracked open, and the contents dripped down his face. He wiped it off with his sleeve.

"Mortimer Proule, I ask you again, how do you plead?"

"Not ruddy guilty. I ain't done nothing, as God's my witness." He sneered at those nearest.

"Not true, not true," cried Mary, leaping up. "He's a liar and a naughty knave."

"Hush your noise, please. This is a court, albeit an unusual one," said Beerson, chomping on a wing that had formerly belonged to a misfortunate bird. Mary plopped back onto the grass, sighing loudly.

"Call Robin Starveling," instructed Winters. Fence gave me a nudge. I took a very small step forward.

"Robin Starveling, did Mortimer Proule strike you so harshly that you fainted?" Winters' face was stern.

"Yes, Admiral," I whispered, shaking a little and taking half a step back.

"Speak up, please. And you have had trouble walking ever since?"

"Yes, Admiral, and also trouble thinking straight on account of a blow to the head."

"You always had trouble thinking straight, you insufferable piece of crap," hissed Scratcher. "Why I came to claim you is a mystery."

"Though I am a little better now than I was at first, true it is," I continued, doing my best to ignore him.

"As God's my witness," said Proule. "I never so much as touched the boy. Ruddy Hell! I want to call a witness."

Winters nodded and Proule turned to the mariner who had been with him that fateful day he'd almost killed me. "Now, John Pickernose, yer was standing right by. I didn't hit the boy, did I?"

"Aye, you did, Master Proule. You thumped 'im black and blue, you clonked 'im proper, to within an inch of 'is life. For fear of God and the admiral, I will not tell a lie." Pickernose bowed to the crowd. The crowd clapped.

Proule roared: "That cockroach Starveling fell over a rock. Pickernose there is a bald-faced liar."

"Am not. You're the liar. If Piggsley and even Boors were here, they'd swear to your villainy on the *Valentine* too. That sailor Timothy Mungle never fell out of the rigging by 'imself. You gave 'im a 'elping 'and cos 'e bested you at dice."

"That's a ruddy lie. And Piggsley and Boors are both swine."

This set the crowd to laughing. "Case proven," said Winters. "Let us move on. Stand before me, Mary Finney."

Mary stood. There were grass stains on her rear.

"Did Mortimer Proule steal your shillings? Do you so charge?"

"He did. And my pouch," she grunted, glaring at Proule. "Them shillings was for my old age, Admiral."

"Huh? You're in your old age now, you crone!" yelled Scratcher. The crowd laughed again. The admiral quelled Scratcher with a look.

"Peter Fence, step forward."

I gave Fence a little push.

"What do you have to say for yourself, young man?" asked Winters.

"I have something for you, sir."

"Pertaining to this case?"

"Aye, sir." Fence drew the crimson pouch from his sleeve and held it up. The crowd gasped.

"That's my property," exclaimed Mary.

"God blind me. He stole it, Admiral. Yer can see for yerself. He stole the shillings too, no doubt about that," said Proule. "He's guilty as sin."

"Then what should I do with him?" asked Winters softly. The crowd hushed.

"Yer should hang him high, Admiral. Hang him high. That's what the law demands, ain't it? And get that cockroach Starveling to pull on his legs. Fence can give him one of them stolen shillings for the service done him in his last moments."

"No mercy?" asked Winters, even more softly.

"No mercy!" grinned Proule, with a terrifying contortion of the face. "No mercy!"

"No mercy," echoed a couple of members of the crowd. Someone punched someone else in the mouth, knocking him out. There was a brief halt in the proceedings as his adversary tried to revive him by jumping on his belly, but Winters soon resumed his questioning.

"Mortimer Proule, the boy entered your hut at my request. Isn't that so, Peter Fence?"

"Aye, sir." Fence blushed. Proule turned as white as ox tripe.

"Where did you find the pouch?" continued Winters.

"Hidden in the tree boughs that formed the roof, sir."

"But no shillings in it?'

"No sir. Not one."

"You are a brave and honest boy. Now go sit down," said Winters.

"Where is the money, Proule?" asked Beerson, having finished eating and dusted bits of roast bird off his nose.

"Yes, where is the goddamned money?" echoed my old master, scratching his ear.

"I'll never tell a man jack of yer," yelled Proule, confirming his guilt.

"Mortimer Proule," said Winters, "the case is proven against you. You prescribed your own punishment when you thought you were sentencing Peter Fence for the same crime, a crime that you, in fact, committed. In addition, the law of England dictates that any man or woman who steals a shilling or more in money or goods shall be put to death. Accordingly, you shall be bound to the tree until tomorrow at ten bells, at which time a rope will be slung over a high bough, and you will be hanged by the neck until dead. Starveling will be employed to pull on your legs. You might think of giving him one of those shillings for his pains."

"Save me, Admiral Winters. Think of what we've been through together, at sea and on land!"

"I am at a loss to know what you mean when you refer to what we've been through together," said Winters. "Speaking for my own part, I have been through very little *with* you, a great deal *without* you, and more than I want to *on account* of you. Take him away."

"Yer tricked me, yer ruddy bastard!" Proule lunged forward and struck Winters full in the face before anyone could stop him. Winters, with surprising strength, knocked him backwards onto the ground. Trusty and Ruffles rushed over, each grabbing one of the villain's legs.

"Where's my shillings, you knock-kneed beast?" shrieked Mary.

"Yer'll never get one of those shillings, never, d'yer hear me? I'll take the secret of where I hid them to the grave," he screamed as the two men dragged him away feet first and set him upright before tying him to the tree close by.

"Stand upon your guard," Winters ordered them. "And wear your weapons at all times."

"Aye, aye, sir," said Trusty or Ruffles, brandishing a stick. One eye, I noticed was staring at Winters, the other at me. It was Ruffles!

"Save me, for the love of God," cried Proule.

"*No mercy*," cried the crowd.

Chapter 33

The Escape

The night had been warm, and I had spent it half in and half out of the lean-to. Tempest had lain across my inside half, his wet nose too near my privates for comfort. He licked the salt on my hose occasionally. He weighed more than a cask of wine. I kept trying to shift him and get my legs out from under, but then he'd climb on Fence, who was curled up inside. Fence would mutter away, still dreaming, about letting the topsail fly and casting something undecipherable into the sea. For the most part his chatter was even more annoying than the dog pressing down on my knees and licking my thighs, so more than once I pulled Tempest off him.

I soon fell back to sleep, but was woken by the rising sun. I blinked. Something small and furry was running across my face. It nipped my ear. A mouse! "Go find cheese or chestnuts," I cried, swatting at it. It ran away.

Climbing all the way out of the lean-to, I stood up

and yawned, stretching my arms. Tempest was chasing the mouse. I looked to see if he'd got it. He seemed to have lost its scent, but something else caught my eye — a crowd had gathered around the tree whereon Proule was tied, and there was an immense hubbub to boot. It couldn't be that the hanging was taking place without me there to pull on Proule's gangly legs. Sunrise was much too early an hour for the execution.

"Fence," I said, ducking my head back in, "Get up quickly, something is happening yonder."

"Down with the mainmast," he mumbled. "Lay her ahold!" Or words to that effect.

"Wake up, will you?" I shook him. "We're not on the ship now."

It took several more shakings, but soon we were on our way to the tree, Fence still tottery and bleary-eyed. He woke up, though, when we reached the scene that was causing so much tumult. Proule's ropes had been cut, and the condemned man was gone.

Winters reached the spot a moment or two after us. He examined the rope before saying, "He couldn't have freed himself. And he was searched quite thoroughly to see if he had any shillings about him. He had not, and he had no weapon either."

"Right sir," said Beerson, who had been standing around praying.

"And those guarding him had sticks, not knives."

"Aye, sir."

"Beerson, that register we made of everyone we brought to the island. Fetch it, if you please, and let us call out the names."

Beerson did so. Everyone was present and responded with an aye, even the shrill-voiced Mary.

"Was there anyone whose name was not called out, who in other words was not on the list?" asked Winters.

I raised my hand. "Me sir, I came later."

"That puts me in mind of remembrancing," said Beerson. "Master Thatcher was not on the list either, sir. He arrived later too."

"Is Thatcher present?" Winters' voice was raised.

Silence. The sun shimmered through the trees. The breeze blew through the leaves. The grass continued to grow a scintilla at a time in its usual fashion. But everything was changed.

"Scratcher could easily have cut the rope. He had a knife, Admiral, a sharp knife he carried always." My voice was high and squeaky. "He used to threaten me with it."

"Beerson," ordered Winters, "take at least six men and search the island for Proule and his dishonourable cohort. If you catch them, they'll both hang."

"Aye, sir, we'll go immediately. As St. Paul said: 'Though I speak with the tongues of men and of angels, and have not charity, I am become as sounding brass, or a tinkling cymb…'"

"Yes, yes," growled Winters, clearly irritated. "Get on with it."

Fence and I didn't wait for the men to hear the rest of their Bible portion before they got organized. Terrified that the two ruffians would find us before being found themselves, we disappeared into the woods instantly, and made for the labyrinth.

Chapter 34

Hidden and Discovered

Five minutes later the dog was bounding after us barking like a fool. "Sh," I said, "shut the hell up, or you'll get us all killed."

He refused to give over. I had a strong urge to kick him, but Fence wanted to try pinching his nose again. This time it worked. I suspect that with life and limb at stake, Fence pinched a lot harder.

"Why would Scratcher be with Proule? Why would he release him? They were fighting like nobody's business the last time they were together," I wondered.

"People make up. We did."

"True it is. But there must be a reason for it. He wouldn't put himself into danger for nothing."

A short distance from the path that led to the labyrinth we heard a rustle and a footfall, and raced to hide in a dense cluster of trees and bushes. We flattened ourselves behind a fallen tree trunk that was covered in moss and fungus. I smelled moldy earth. Inhaling some of it, I smothered a cough. Fence clamped his hand over the dog's jaws and pushed the animal's shoulders down so that the rest of him followed. Tempest whined a little, but couldn't get his mouth open to bark.

"What's that noise?" someone said, voice muffled.

"Nothing. Or something. Beasts of the forest, more'n likely. Damned if I know where we are, or where we ain't, Scratcher." A familiar odour assailed my nostrils. It beat out the moldy smell by a mile. It was Proule! He must be almost as close to me as I was to Fence. I hardly dared breathe. Nor, frankly, did I want to. The stench was horrible.

"Don't call me Scratcher, you demented son of a gorilla."

A mumbled apology. Another rustle. We ducked down even further. A twig grazed my nose.

"I'm no fool. You're playing me. Give me my half, and be quick about it," yelled Scratcher. Half of what? Hell's Bells. Half of the shillings, of course. That's why Scratcher had set Proule free.

"Yer'll get it, no worries. I buried the booty by a ruddy great rock. We just need to find it. The commotion of the trial has driven where it lies straight out of my head. All I know right now is where it ain't. It ain't here."

They passed by in a cloud of Proule's stink, chuntering at each other while Tempest growled soft and deep in his throat. They left a smelly residue behind them, so we couldn't be sure they were gone and looked both ways before emerging from our hideout. I coughed profusely. Then we found the path, and rushed along it to the entrance of the labyrinth. Near the end, Tempest, who kept getting in the way in his doggy fashion, jumped in front of my feet, tripping me, and I lurched into Fence. All three of us collapsed in a sorry tangle.

"Welcome," said the old man with the white beard as we tried, somewhat unsuccessfully, to unscramble ourselves. "I knew you were beset by enemies. I thought you might return." He pulled the dog off us, helped us up, and ushered us in. I noticed his feet. They were pretty big. But what choice did we have?

Chapter 35

Entering by Invitation

Beneath the sky lay the labyrinth. Beyond the labyrinth was the shore, its secret sand script washed away by the tide. Above the shore were the rocks, and beyond the rocks was the cave. Under the earth a bed stood by the wall, and a throne-like chair filled the space between the entrance and the bed. A huge fire burned in the grate within a circle of rocks. All in the cave, in fact, was exactly as it had been before, with one exception: The gold medallion, winking precious gems on its glittering chain, was gone.

"Well, you surely didn't think I'd keep it in plain view knowing you wanted to steal it? It was on the chair because I had been polishing it, not expecting company; not immediately, anyway. When I realized you would probably come again, I put it somewhere safe. I thought it best to keep you and temptation as far from each other as possible." Fence had been right. The man had heard him and me arguing about it. My heart beat fast and loud.

"Who are you both?"

"Peter Fence, sir, at your service. We were shipwrecked here with other voyagers on our way to Virginia."

I considered for a moment. "Robin Starveling. We ran here to avoid a pair of ruffians who didn't have our best interests at heart."

"The name doesn't seem to belong to you. Is it what you were christened?" The old man's voice was sharp.

"No, sir, it was given me by my master. My real name is … my real name is…." but whether from trepidation or excitement my real name had turned tail and fled back to Plymouth. "It's been so long since I went by it, I've forgotten," I admitted.

The man seemed to understand. He said nought else, but threw something sparkly on the fire. With a crackle and a hiss, it flared up. Light fled through the hole in the roof. Shadows like rearing beasts licked the walls. Perhaps he really was magical. I was greatly afeard, and Fence was also. I could see his hands and toes trembling. The man cracked his fingers loudly. We shrank back.

"Come now, boys, there's nothing to be frightened of. My bones are stiff and I have the rheumatics, that's all. The two of you haven't escaped two villains simply to find yourself in the clutches of a third."

"Is he a wizard?" Fence whispered.

"A wizard? No, not I, though I know a trick or two and I have very good hearing."

"But what about the glimmering spiders' webs…?" said I.

"That is the island's own magic, not mine." He laughed long and hard in his creaky way and tossed a new log on the flames. Bringing us both a mixture of crushed berries in water, he bade us drink, before seating himself on the stone chair.

"Take a long draught. It's good. Take another. You are still here," he went on, "because I want you to be. In fact, I was about to reveal myself to you, but you, brilliant boys that you are, found me all by yourselves."

"Well, but we were helped by the ciphers, sir."

"What ciphers would those be?"

"The ciphers in the emblems that gave us the clues to your whereabouts."

"I know of no ciphers. Unless you mean the small one in the sand."

"No sir, although I would like to know what it said."

"I've forgotten. Or at least, it is of no moment now." He stood for a moment deep in thought. "But come to think of it, I know where those other ciphers must have come from."

"Scratcher said they were from a famous emblem maker, sir."

"And that makes perfect sense." He didn't explain further. "I first caught sight of you on the other island. I could tell people had come, the hammering and shouting echoed all the way from there to here. Besides, wreckage from the ship was washing up on this island too. I'd hollowed a small tree trunk into a boat to travel short distances in, so I went across. I spied the two of you poring over papers in the forest."

"Those would have been the emblems, sir." I remembered the creepy feeling of being watched while we were in the spinney. But, "Why did you wait? Why didn't you just reveal yourself right then, to everyone?" I asked.

"All in good time."

"But there is no treasure? There is just you?" I burst out, disappointed.

"There is and there isn't treasure, Robin Starveling. There are two sides to everything. It depends on which side you look at." He got up and ambled around as if searching for something, before poking the fire with a stick so that bright red embers flew up. Disappearing for a moment into one of the cave's many recesses, he returned with two large palm leaves. "These shall be your blankets. Sleep now. I shall not harm you. You are perfectly safe here, underground."

Sleep we did, long and dreamlessly, the dread and distress of past weeks seeping slowly away. I wasn't sure we could trust him, but my eyes were closing in spite of my best efforts to keep them open. The drink must have contained a sleeping potion.

"Yes," he agreed the next day, when I finally had the courage to ask him. "The berries are from a special scarlet and gold-leaved tree, which I call the sleeping tree. They give rest to those who are most weary, but they aren't harmful. I told you I knew a trick or two, and I do."

Chapter 36

Bastard Prince

For about two days we stayed with him. It was hard to tell the passing of time in a place where there was no window and neither sunlight nor moonshade. We thought he held us by magic, but it was more likely naught to do with him. It was our feeling of security there, and our fear of venturing forth again. We had escaped our two worst enemies, Proule and Scratcher, after all. Now we were in the cave I felt they could never bother us again. As to where they now were, I had no clue. Nor did I much care.

The man gave us more food and drink, and led us to a spring which flowed down the rocks in a recess of the cave. Fence and I washed ourselves, splashing water on each other and the dog while the man left us alone. In fact he left us alone most of the time. Every now and then, though, I caught him staring at us. He's sizing us up, I thought, for degrees of goodness and wickedness. Fence was at one end of the scale. I knew only too well I was at the other. Occasionally what the old man thought mattered a lot to me. At other times it didn't seem to matter at all.

He was a conundrum. An *enigma*, Witch Oldham would say. "He knew I wanted to nick the medallion from him, but he didn't turn a hair," I said to Fence. "Most adults threaten me, slap me, or drag me around by the ear. And that's when I'm behaving."

"But we still don't know who he is or how he got here," he whispered. "Are we right to trust him?"

"All will be revealed in due course," called the man, from an unseen corner of the cave, his hearing sharper than Tempest's. "When, Peter Fence, I know your friend has wiped his pilfering fingers clean and I can trust you both."

"Oh, but you can," I said, although I crossed those same fingers because I didn't know for sure that I was telling the truth. I did not choose to live with wickedness, after all. On the contrary, like Tempest the shaggy mutt, it chose to live with me.

But he must have believed my protestations, because on the second day he sat down with us and commenced a story.

"*There was once a boy. He lived in the country with a poor peasant family that he believed was his own. It was the only family he ever remembered having. The people he thought to be his parents were kind to him, and the man he called father taught him to read in the evenings, as the monks had taught the father years before. During the day, the boy worked out in the fields, sowing, reaping, helping bring in the harvest, and tending the family's animals."*

"Just like me," interrupted Fence. "I looked after the sheep. Did the boy's father die, like mine did?"

"*No, he stayed hearty and hale. But one day a very well-dressed man on a white steed came to the family's little house. He was leading a pony. 'You will pack your clothing,' he told the boy. 'I am here to take you to school.' The boy had no idea who the rich man was, but the woman he called mother encouraged him to go, though she was crying. 'He is a trustworthy man. You must do as he tells you. Perhaps all will be explained.'*

"*The boy had little to pack as he was so poor. The man put him astride the pony, and they started on a long journey. It was very difficult for him because he'd never ridden before and his legs soon became sore and cramped. He was also homesick. On their way to the school they came to a great castle. 'We will stop here,' the man said. He took the boy inside. Servants led him into a huge hall. A woman soon entered. She was dressed in magnificent silver and black robes and wore a coronet on her bright red hair. 'Remember always who you are,' she told the boy, as if he should know who that was. Taking a pendant from her neck, she placed it around his. It was a Phoenix pendant. 'I am the Phoenix,' she said. The boy had no idea what she meant."*

The old man put his hand to his throat. That's where the medallion is, I thought. Around his own neck. Under his clothes. He is wearing it.

"The bird that dies and is burnt, then rises from its own ashes," I said aloud. "I thought I recognized it. Who was the woman?" I believed I already knew who he was going to name.

"*She was Elizabeth, Queen of England, though the boy didn't find out until later. 'You are her son,' said the man taking him to school, 'the son of her majesty and Robert Dudley, one of her favourites, but you must never tell anyone or it may destroy the monarchy. She is known to her subjects as the Virgin Queen. That's why she couldn't keep you in the palace. That's why she sent you away. Your real name is Arthur Dudley. But you will go by your old name in school.' And so he did.*"

"I have two names too, true it is." I had remembered my old name, but Noah Vaile didn't seem to fit me any longer, so I didn't mention it.

"*The boy never saw the Queen again. He carried his old name through school, through university, and out to sea, on his way to Italy. But then, in a terrible storm, he was shipwrecked and taken up by a Spanish ship. The English were at war with the Spanish, but luckily the boy, who was now a young man, had learned to speak and write Latin. 'What is your name?' they asked him in that language. 'Tell us the truth or we will torture you for the spy that you are.'*

So for the first time, he revealed his true name: 'I am Arthur Dudley, son to the Queen of England; therefore, you must not harm me.'

"*'I have never heard of you. Are you her heir?' someone asked him.*

"*The idea had never occurred to him before, so he thought about it for some moments before replying. 'I am the true heir, as I was born to her majesty. To my knowledge, she has had no other children.'*

"*'Are you a bastard?'*

"*'I know not whether she was married to my father, Robert Dudley, the earl of Leicester, but it matters little, as I am blood of her blood and heir of her body. She is not the consort or mistress of a king. She is Queen in her own right.'*

"*'He is very valuable to us,' said the captain, who had listened carefully. 'Soon we will launch the Armada and vanquish the English. Perhaps we can train Dudley to replace Elizabeth as the new sovereign of England. Unknown to the people, he will report to us. The English will accept him once she is gone, as he is of the same blood as the Queen.'*

"*The captain took Arthur Dudley back to Spain. The Spanish King decided to send him to a Catholic Mission in the Americas, to be instructed in the faith and so that he could be hidden until the Spaniards were victorious. But in a strange twist of fate there was a second shipwreck on the way to the New World, and the young man was cast up on these isles.*"

"Just like us," said Peter Fence.

"Except that he was alone. Everyone else went down with the ship, but young and hearty as he was, he was strong enough to swim to shore. While exploring the islands, he found a cave, and set to work to make it comfortable and construct the paths around it, hidden paths that led out to the sea, so he could see if anyone came without their seeing him, and to make a habitation fit for a prince. He remembered that many of the great houses of England had labyrinths, so he built one for himself to confuse travellers. That way, no one would find him, and he would only venture to identify himself when it was safe to do so. Most sincerely, he wished not to fall back into Spanish hands. But as time went on he became more and more lonely and wondered why he alone had been saved.

"Years later a French boat was shipwrecked on the rocks nearby, with an Englishman, Henricus Plumsell, a famous emblem and verse maker, and many Frenchmen on board. After watching them for several weeks, Arthur deemed them safe and went to meet them. He became friends with Plumsell, and took him back to the cave, where he told him his story. When the French built a small pinnace from pieces of wreckage and the planks of the island's trees to carry them home, he begged to be taken off the island and travel with them so that he might return to England.

"'The boat is too small,' said the French captain. 'I barely know how we will transport our own people. And then there's Monsieur Plumsell to consider. I've already picked him up

from another wreck. I don't wish many English on board. They make me uneasy. One is acceptable, two are conspirators.' Arthur begged and pleaded, but it availed him not. 'We did not bring you here, and we shall not take you hence,' insisted the captain.

"*'I could stow away,' he told Plumsell privately, 'if you would help me by sharing your food so I don't starve during the journey.'*

"*'It would be more than my life's worth. And if you were found, which would be very likely on such a small ship, you'd be thrown headlong into the ocean, hundreds of miles away from anywhere, and I would too. These men have few scruples, especially when their own lives might be in danger.'*"

By now I knew well enough who the young man was, of course, but I said nothing. Fence, not the sharpest knife in the drawer, was sitting slack jawed and open mouthed.

"*Heartbroken, the young man returned to the cave and tried to think of a plan. Just before the pinnace left, he gave Plumsell a note written in his own blood on a large palm leaf, and asked him to deliver it to the Queen so that she would send an expedition in search of him. Plumsell took the note and tucked it into his doublet. He didn't agree to deliver it, but he didn't say he wouldn't, either.*

"*Now in essence, it wasn't up to Arthur, it was up to Plumsell, and more important, to Dame Fortune herself. Whenever Arthur thought of Dame Fortune, he saw her dressed as the Queen had been dressed on the one occasion he had been brought into her royal presence, in magnificent black and silver robes, with flaming hair and a coronet. She was his Dame Fortune."*

He stood up. The cave was full of shadows. "I was that boy. I was that young man. I am Arthur Dudley, son to the Queen of England. And now you have found me. Or at least, we have found one another."

Chapter 37

On His Head the Crown?

Fence gasped. "You are the son of the Queen? You, yourself?" Tempest was running around in circles chasing his tail as though he'd just discovered he had one.

"Yes I am."

"So the crown in the cipher text represents you?" I was trembling.

"I believe it must. Plumsell must have composed the ciphers in hopes they would draw people here. He was an expert emblem and cipher maker. Perhaps he went to the Queen but she wouldn't help. After all, she acknowledged my existence only once, and only in private. Plumsell was the only person besides myself who knew the way to the cave."

"He never published them though. They were still in manuscript."

"That is a mystery. Perhaps he decided it was too dangerous to his own safety to publish what amounted to a treasure map to a crown prince of England. But it accounts for the fact that no one, until you boys, ever found me."

"Admiral Winters says that the Isle of Devils is a terrible place for storms and shipwrecks," said Fence. "That might also be a reason."

"Just so. It's possible many may have set out, but to my knowledge no one ever reached here. I wonder if Plumsell ever did take my letter to the Queen. It would be a risky thing to do."

Fence looked dumbfounded, and true it is, I was stunned myself. Amazement had been growing in me since the beginning of Dudley's story. Here was I, Robin Starveling, not pinching pies any longer, but perchance standing next to real honest to goodness English royalty. If things went right I would be set up for life. *Prince Arthur and his entourage*, I thought. That would definitely include me. But there were a few obstacles to overcome. First, I had to be certain in my mind that he was who he said he was. There were plenty of people around who were as barking mad — or perhaps I should say oinking mad — as Boors. And with Dudley there was, for example, the minor problem of the pronoun. "It's a strange story, true enough. But why do you refer to yourself as 'he' and 'him'?" I asked.

"It is all so long ago and far away. It seems to have happened to another man. I think of it almost as a fairy tale."

Good answer, I thought. Chalk one up for the Prince.

Fence blinked, then rubbed his nose thoughtfully. "Queen Elizabeth died more than six years ago. James of Scotland is King of England now."

"I never thought of that possibility," Dudley cried. "I imagined my mother still alive." He threw his hands over his face, but after a moment he composed himself, let his hands fall to his sides, and drew himself up to his full height. "I cannot mourn her. I did not know her. But good God, if the Queen is dead and has been all these years, it is a fairy tale no longer." Suddenly he didn't look as old, and his bearing was regal. "I never thought to see this day. I have long been Island King, but I ruled no one but myself. Now, as James is no more than distant cousin to the late Queen, I am the true King of England."

I gulped. This was even more exciting. It was like watching a play. But it was perilous too. Who would dare to tell James he was not the real King? And what would happen then?

"Hoorah," cried Fence, wrapped up in measureless content.

"James of Scotland is a fraud and a usurper. I must return right away to London and claim my rightful place as the son of the Queen. Are you with me?"

"Aye, aye, your majesty," said Fence, saluting him. I saluted him too, though more than a bit nervously. A rebellion could prove very dangerous, and I preferred to keep my head connected to the rest of me.

"We must tell no one here and go with stealth. I don't want to run the risk of waiting longer, or being left on the island again by someone who might not believe me King, someone who would perchance consider me a lunatic or a traitor."

Winters might well think that, I realized. "Is that why you didn't reveal yourself right away to everyone?"

"Yes. I had to make sure that the people who found me, or perhaps it would be truer to say whom I found, were of trustworthy natures. Not like your old and vicious master and his crony. As with the French ship, I bided my time."

I put my right hand behind my back and crossed my fingers. One thing I wasn't was trustworthy. Not that it was my fault. It was the hand fate had dealt me.

"You might like gold, Robin Starveling, but from what I've seen of you when you're with Peter Fence, I'd say you are a trusty friend and a loyal ally."

"He is a right good'un, sire," said Fence.

Dudley smiled. "We will raise an army when we reach England. There is the small matter of a ship," he mused, who despite what others such as Winters might think, appeared to be turning into a monarch before my very eyes. This was all happening a bit too fast. I couldn't believe he'd be able to raise an army. But although I'd had no time to consider it, I was pretty sure his story must be true. There wasn't a trace of the madman about him, except perchance in his idea that he and a ragtaggle group armed with pikes and pitchforks could defeat King James. And he did possess the Phoenix Medallion, which was to my mind the clincher that he was the son of the late Queen. He didn't have shifty eyes like Proule, or a deceitful air like Scratcher. He hadn't stolen it, I was certain now. But others might not be. And whether he wanted to go raise an army or not, I still believed our best bet was to get off the island first, and make decisions later. I had plenty of time, while we were sailing back to England, to try to change his mind if need be.

"I do feel that with some judicious planning we might work out where we could find a boat, sire," said I, his new minister in waiting, "as your hollow tree trunk sounds much too small to carry us all." There were two boats anchored close to shore. The pinnace had been built by Winters and his men, while the rowboat had been commandeered by Scratcher. The rowboat wouldn't get us very far and I would be terrified enough at sea without trying to outmanoeuvre the waves in a craft the size of a soup bowl. No, we would steal the pinnace, the pinnace that was meant to carry Winters to Virginia sometime soon. Swiping what belonged to others, was, you might say, my stock-in-trade.

Chapter 38

Out of the Cave and into Danger

I poked my head out of the cave. It was growing late, and would be twilight soon enough, so I beckoned to the others. Tempest immediately rushed out, turned right, and got lost; that is, lost to us. I'm sure he knew where he was. It just didn't happen to be where we were. In a moment, Fence and Arthur Dudley slipped out and joined me, and we made our way through the labyrinth. Dudley was carrying a large sack of supplies, and Fence carried a lantern.

Soon we were treading quickly along the path that led towards camp, with me leading the way. We would skirt the settlement and head for the makeshift harbour. I was just imagining a cherry pie, its pastry brown and crisp, loaded with mountains of whipped cream fresh from the cow — funny it is, how I always think about food at the most inopportune times — when we ran smack into Scratcher and Proule. Or at least, we came within spitting distance of them. We quickly ducked behind palms, but the trees were spindly and didn't afford even such as us much cover.

For once, the two men were not making a sound. They were fighting, locked in a grim embrace. Behind them glittered a handful of shillings. The money sat between a small hole and a large rock. They must have just dug it up, or been about to bury it again. "Quick," I whispered to Fence. "Take the cash and run. We'll meet up later."

"It's not ours."

"Now's not the time for goddamn philosophical discussions. Pick up the money and get. I'll follow as quickly as I can, but have Dudley to think of. Misfortunately he can't move fast."

Scratcher and Proule had been in deadly combat for Scratcher's knife, but Proule must have heard us, and me especially, for as he fought on he fixed the tree behind which I hid with a demonic glare. My knees wobbled with fear and I almost fell over. I was probably the only person in the world he hated more than Scratcher. With a guttural shout he punched his opponent hard with his free hand, while violently jerking the knife out of Scratcher's fingers. He lunged towards the tree, circling round it so that he was directly in front of me. "Say yer prayers, cockroach, yer traitorous bug, because I'm dispatching yer to heaven or hell right now. Then I'll take care of Scratcher."

"Don't call me that," screeched his opponent, near crazed with rage.

Proule rushed at me. Dudley, seeing my danger, dumped his sack and thrust himself between Proule's body and mine. "Leave the boy alone. He's under my protection," Dudley rasped in his rusty-key voice. But the knife, which was meant for me, slid fast and sharp into him instead. He went down, first onto his knees, then onto his side. I cried out. Proule was thrown off balance for a moment and staggered backwards into the tree.

"No!" he yelled, for despite their earlier fearful and most dreadful struggle, Scratcher now had the advantage and was closing on the knife. With a savage wrench he pulled it out of Dudley. The old man moaned before falling silent. His chest and arm were covered with blood. Horrified, I knelt down next to him. For once I didn't care about my own safety. I had brought him to this.

Swinging around, as if performing a courtly dance, Scratcher whooped in triumph. He pinned Proule with the knife and plunged it deep into his belly. Then he twisted the blade. Proule shrieked and fell forward onto earth and grass, landing at Scratcher's feet. His head hit first, the impact pushing it around and up so that at least one eye still glared at me. The knife handle stuck out of his stomach at an angle, preventing him from falling flat, but he appeared quite, quite, dead.

"Waste of a good knife," complained Scratcher. He turned Proule over and tried to retrieve it a couple of times After a third attempt, finding it was still jammed fast, he spat on the ground and kicked the body. Then he tacked towards the hole and the rock.

"Where are the bloody shillings?" he screamed. "God's Blood, where are they? They're mine, and mine alone," He didn't care about anything or anyone else, not even about who Dudley was, or rather, who Dudley had been. Not even that Proule was dead. Not even that Scratcher himself was a murderer. "The coins were right here. I killed Proule on account of them and now they're gone." With a whoop he realized Fence wasn't there either. "That foul coward of a cabinboy was here just a moment ago. I saw him. He must have taken off with them." In a trice Scratcher disappeared after Fence.

My heart hammered. Should I go or should I stay here? I would run to find Fence, and try to keep us both out of harm's way, but I had something to do first, something that couldn't wait.

I was still kneeling next to Dudley, my tears falling onto his robes. Here was the only man besides Piggsley who had ever shown any kindness to me. Here was possibly the true King of England. He had saved my life. He lay dead on the ground. I crossed myself and cried even harder. But I had to accomplish my horrid task. Gritting my teeth, I reached beneath the neckband of his bloodstained robes until I felt something cold. A heavy chain. Lifting his head, I began to pull the loop of gold off him, sobbing all the while. The Phoenix Medallion. It was mine at last, but I didn't feel in the least triumphant. True it is, I felt like a traitor, but told myself that this was fair play, even by Fence's rules, as it could not be said to belong to Dudley any longer. But I never got it completely off him. Sure though I was that Dudley was dead, it turned out that he wasn't. His eyes opened and he grimaced.

I couldn't believe it. "Sire, you're alive," I managed to mutter, stupidly enough, before letting the medallion drop so it was truly his again.

He groaned. "Just barely. The demon thought he got me in the heart, but it was my arm. It bleeds apace. Tear off the hem of my robe."

I did so with some difficulty.

"Now wrap it tightly as you can around my left arm."

I did as I was told, thinking all the while how close his arm was to his heart, and how easily he might have been slaughtered. But as I helped him to his feet, I saw something move out of the corner of my eye.

Hell's Bells and buckets of blood. It was Proule. He staggered up and started towards us, both hands wrapped around the knife handle. He was attempting to pull it out of his own belly, no doubt so he could stick it in mine. A strange gurgling sound was coming from his throat. "I've … got … yer … now, Cockroach."

His mouth opened wide. I could see every blackened tooth in his head. I screamed.

Chapter 39

Keeping the Treasure

I took off in a panic, half leading, half dragging Dudley. He had saved my life. Now I must save his. But though we travelled at a snail's pace, Proule was even slower and we soon left him behind. Finally I thought I heard him slam back down. Somewhere in the deep woods, Tempest barked. Then there was silence.

As we limped towards the shore, I took care to keep an eye open for Scratcher while I looked for Fence in our secret places in the forest. But Fence was nowhere to be found. We finally discovered him down by the boats, by which time, in my mind at least, he'd died a hundred different deaths. And so had I. In my imagination I saw Proule or Scratcher advancing towards me, knife raised. But whoever had the knife, the vision always ended the same way. I was killed in some barbaric manner in the dead of night, leaving Dudley alone and unprotected. But now, as we came to the shore, it was dawn. The sky cracked red as the orange sun rose through the canopy of trees.

"Thanks be. Did Scratcher find you?" I asked Fence.

"No." He was panting. "Would I be here if he did? I heard someone crashing through the trees and quickly snuffed out the light. 'My shillings, my shillings,' he shrieked, before stumbling on again. 'I'll get you, see if I don't.' It was Scratcher, right enough. I was greatly afraid. But I never saw him, and he didn't catch sight of me. God save us, what's wrong with his majesty?"

"Hurry, help me get him into the pinnace. He was stabbed in the arm trying to keep me from harm." I smothered my sobs with a cough.

"I have something I must tell you, Robin, before we leave."

"What? Not now. Take his other arm. Quickly. We need to get him on board so he can lie down. He's lost a barrelful of blood."

Fence grabbed Dudley and we splashed our way out to the boat.

I struggled into it, hauling Dudley in after me as if he were a catch of fish. For such a slight man he was a ton weight. Fence slung himself over the rail and we laid the old man, who seemed asleep, on the deck.

"I don't have the shillings," Fence admitted now we'd settled Dudley as best we could. "I left them in Mary's hut, in her red pouch, while she slept. It was the honest thing to do."

"No matter. She can have her ill-gotten gains." We had saved Dudley, which was worth so much more to me. I was now untying a rope, which seemed to me to be the sailorly thing to do. But I was still a mere apprentice in matters seafaring.

"They'd be more ill-gotten if *we* kept them. But I thought you'd kill me."

"True it is, I'm glad to see you. There's been so much bloodletting that I thought I might not. And we have inherited, you might say, something far better than a few measly shillings. We have Dudley. We have his trust. And he has the Phoenix medallion. Wherever we end up, he'll look after us, and we him."

Fence retied the rope. "Right you are. Just do what I tell you, Robin, as regards shipshapery, and don't mess with the shrouds without permission, lest we sink."

That told me off, good and proper. "Aye, aye, sir."

"Take hold of that chain," he instructed, so I did.

As we made preparation to get underway, I related everything that had happened. When he heard how Dudley had nearly been killed, he wept quietly as he worked.

"But, if Proule has died," he said after a few minutes, "and Scratcher is off in the woods, no doubt terrified of what the others will do if they find him, why need we go at all? And what right do we have to take the boat?"

"Proule, I'm pretty sure, is dead as a doornail." I shivered at the thought of him tottering towards me, blood dripping, knife stuck and twisted in his belly as he tried fruitlessly to pull it out. No one could survive such a grave wound to the innards, not for long, anyway. And if he did succeed in pulling the knife out, he would bleed to death, like a stuck pig, all the faster. "But Scratcher is another matter. He's still alive, he's desperate, and he has nothing to lose. And we're the witnesses to his cowardly doings, remember." I still imagined him behind every tree, every rock, ready to spring forward and kill us. Even Winters might not be able to stop him. His hatred ran too deep. I had bested him, after all. "And for the love of God don't complain that we'll be stealing the boat. We have no choice if we want to live till Easter. And we have Dudley aboard. He would order us to commandeer it if he were awake. So we'll pretend he has done just that."

Fence took up the ropes again. "Aye. It will be a hard trip, Robin, even though the pinnace is well set up. A boat with one mast can be almost as difficult to handle as one with three, mayhap more so, as it doesn't have the weight. We'll get tossed around something awful. We won't get a wink of sleep. And we'll have to look after his majesty. Pray God he makes it through the voyage."

"He will. He says it is only a flesh wound."

"He can talk then?"

"Yes. A little. Never mind the dangers." I tried to sound brave, though I knew I'd soon feel green as a salad on account of the waves. "We'll manage somehow. You'll teach me the ropes, as you said."

"My glove!" Fence exclaimed suddenly. "It's still on Boors Island."

"We can't stop for it. Fence my boy. When we reach England, I'll buy you an entire pair of gloves."

"Thank you, Robin."

"And if I haven't the cash to buy them straight off, I'll pinch them off a barrow."

Fence made a face, but then laughed aloud, used as he had become to my roguish ways.

"Which way will we go?" I asked.

"West, then north along the coast, past Virginia, thence to Newfoundland, where with luck we might get picked up by an English fishing boat, and then home. His majesty will have to stay disguised. He will have to remain plain Arthur Dudley. Pray for a fair wind."

"Aye, aye, cap'n!" We'd swapped places. Fence was my gov'nor now. I judged it the wrong time to tell him that England might not be the place to go if we wanted to keep our heads. Perhaps we would find a home in Jamestown, Virginia, or somewhere north of it, even Newfoundland.

As we hoisted the sails, I saw movement in the trees beyond the shore, and my heart lurched. But it was only that stupid mutt Tempest. He piddled twice, bounded across the sand, dog paddled through a few feet of water, and barked to be pulled up.

"I hope you'll be our only tempest on this voyage," Fence told him, as he lifted him into the boat in a bucket.

"Amen to that," said I, grinning like an idiot. But a mile or so underway, with me bathing Dudley's head with sea water, Fence, who was a devil for remembering, suddenly yelled, "The supplies are still in the forest. We have to go back."

"And be caught by Scratcher? Not on your life. We've a pail to catch rainwater and we'll fish, at least until I think of something better." Not that I knew how we'd fish without rod or net. Or when it would rain, if at all. The sky had turned from orangey red to a piercing blue.

But as luck would have it, as we passed Boor's Island, we saw a man, his face half hidden by a cap. We dipped beneath the rail, but after a moment I took a quick squint. It was our old friend Piggsley, searching for crabs by the rocks. I stood up and he waved to us. With no little trouble we steered the ship close to the shore. I splashed over to him and told him our tale — well, a goodish part of it, anyway. I thought it best not to mention that the old man we'd brought with us either was, or thought he was, the King of England. Piggsley considered for a moment before saying that he wanted to come along. "Not doing anything worth a piss in a pot here, Ginger Top. And Boors be'ant fit to be in charge, the mad blighter. No worries about food, laddies. We s'll stay close to land when we can and we s'll find it as we goes."

"One second," I said. I ran into the spinney to dig out Fence's glove before Piggsley and I waded back to the pinnace.

"Here be some seafood to start us off," said Piggsley. He threw the crabs he'd caught onto the deck, and Tempest, stupid brute that he was, tracked one till it turned around and pincered him on the nose. It was much harder than Fence had ever pinched him. It was as hard as when St. Dunstan pinched the Devil's nose with red hot tongs. In spite of everything, I laughed as I knocked the crab off the cur's much beleaguered snout. He yelped and crawled to the prow.

"And if we hugs the land," Piggsley went on, "we s'll find some fine tortoises around the coast a piece. Jes' one of'em'll keep us fed while we's crossing nor'west to the shores of Virginie. Fresh water up that way, too."

"And after that?" I asked.

"If the winds be kind, we s'll stop in at Jamestown, where we was first headed. To see if the streets be really paved with gold." He winked. "And there too we s'll load up with provisions before going on."

"And if the winds aren't kind?"

"If they be'ant kind we s'll hole up on an island somewhere. At least we s'll be our own men, none of that bowin' and scrapin' and eternal catchin' of flies both seen and not seen, for Sir Thomas Boors."

"We now have an expert in all things nautical," I said, pleased. "Not discounting Peter Fence, of course. No offence meant, Fence."

Fence was busy stretching the fingers of his salt-stained glove before pulling it on. "None taken, Robin. Please take command, Master Piggsley." He saluted.

"Much obliged to you, Master Fence. You s'll make a fine first mate." As Piggsley put his hand to the tiller, he began to sing:

I sees a wreck to windward,
And a lofty ship to lee,
A sailing down all on the coasts
But on sails we.

Look ahead, look astern,
Look the weather in the lee,
Blow high, blow low,
As on sails we.

Pull, pull me hearties,
All on the glitt'ring sea
The sails be full, the shrouds be taut
And on sails we…

"Bound for England," shouted Fence. "Or if not England, then somewhere else. As long as we all stay together."

"Yes, as long as we all stay together," echoed a rusty voice behind us. It was Dudley. "I still hope to get to England, but it is no longer my first concern. I have been too long alone to deny myself the comfort of companionship."

I was greatly relieved. Mayhap the seepings of his own blood with their whispery omens of death had changed his thinking.

"We'll be fine," I said, "just as long as we stay above the waves." I was already beginning to gasp at the ups and downs of the boat, and had a whirligging in my bonce. I was feeling right greenish, as Fence would say. But true it is, I was also beginning to feel the faintest tickle of pleasure that ran all the way along my spine to my toes. We were sailing past the rocks near the Bermudas without hurt or hurricano. We had beaten those savage tripeheads, Proule and Scratcher. And even if Scratcher was still in the forest chuntering to himself that he would get us in the end, so what? We'd left him far behind, the worst devil in the Isle of Devils. Soon, if the weather stayed fair, there would be hundreds of miles of ocean between us. And for the first time in my life I had real friends, companions who were as good as or better than family.

Thus set off the strangest crew that ever sailed the seven seas: an old mariner with a kind heart and a trunkful of seafaring experience; a young rapscallion with a whoosh of wickedness about him who could finagle his way out of any tight spot (when not feeling like to puke); an honest cabin boy who was loyal and strong and would work till his hands blistered; a loud-mouthed mongrel (the less said about him the better); and of course, a wise king who, when recovered, would guide us all. It occurred to me there and then that if we didn't make it to England (and I rather hoped we wouldn't), we had everything necessary for a thriving colony on some undiscovered island or the long coast of Virginia. Much heartened, I began to sing along with Piggsley. Fence, Tempest, and a quavering Dudley joined in the chorus, as *on sailed we.*

Author's Note

In June 1609, a fleet of ships known as the Third Supply departed England for Jamestown, Virginia. On the way they encountered a terrible hurricane. One ship, the *Sea Venture*, was cast away on the Bermuda Islands, long known to be a place of fearful storms and shipwrecks. Amazingly, there was no loss of life and several months later, after building two pinnaces (small boats), the crew and passengers managed to reach Virginia. From there many returned to England to tell their miraculous tale. Various witnesses wrote about the experience, and their stories were published in 1610 and later. In 1625, *A True Reportory of the Wreck and Redemption of Sir Thomas Gates, Knight, upon and from the Islands of the Bermudas*, by William Strachey, who had been "a sufferer and an eye witness" in Bermuda, was published in a large volume with many other narratives.

It has been theorized, but certainly not proven, that Shakespeare saw *True Reportory* in manuscript, whereupon it became a source for *The Tempest*. Unfortunately *True Reportory*, although purporting to be entirely factual, borrows much of its detail from other earlier travellers' tales and works of fiction that were also available to Shakespeare. It is, however, a wonderful yarn.

Minerva's Voyage is very loosely based on Strachey's narrative, although it veers away from it as the novel progresses. Many names, including the name of the ship, have been changed, and most characters, including Robin Starveling himself — his name comes from Shakespeare's *A Midsummer Night's Dream* — are fictional. Since Strachey seems to have borrowed much and changed truth to fiction in his work, I felt it no shame to do likewise.

In 1587, many years before the wreck of the *Sea Venture*, a young Englishman travelling abroad told Sir Francis Englefield, who had the ear of King Philip II of Spain, that his name was Arthur Dudley. He further said that he was the son of Queen Elizabeth I of England, by Sir Robert Dudley, a favourite of the Queen's. Arthur disappeared shortly after the defeat of the Spanish Armada, and was never heard from again. I have invented the rest of his story to suit my novel and its sequel, which I'm beginning to work on now.

There is, by the way, an unsolved cipher in Chapter 23 and another in Chapter 29. There is one other secret message in the book, but if you're interested in decoding it, you'll have to find it for yourself. Happy hunting!

Lynne Kositsky

Acknowledgements

Many thanks to my husband Michael and son Adam, who helped out, were exceedingly patient, and brought me numerous cups of tea,

To the rest of my supportive family,

To my super agent, Margaret Hart, who works tirelessly on my behalf, and to her staff,

To Michael Carroll and all his staff at Dundurn, for accepting and publishing *Minerva's Voyage*,

To my kind and generous copy editor, Cheryl Hawley,

To Professor Roger Stritmatter of Coppin State University, Maryland, who worked with me to produce a series of academic articles on the Bermuda narratives and *The Tempest*, and came up with the title of the novel based on them,

To Professor Timothy Billings of Middlebury College, Vermont, who has a phenomenal website and kindly gave me permission to use images from *Minerva Britanna* in my book,

To Tom Reedy, an expert on William Strachey,

To Martin Hyatt, who supplied research papers from EEBO and elsewhere that I needed,

To Sean Phillips, who showed me the backstreet (but legal) way to access JSTOR and the OED,

To Ted Alexander, who patiently gave me advice and fixed my computer every time it crashed,

To Barbara Berson, who took the trouble to review the text,

To my dear friend Charis Wahl, who discussed the book with me on numerous occasions while plying me with dim sum,

To the late and much missed K.C. Ligon of New York, who was my sounding board on too many occasions to count,

To all my other friends, writerly, neighbourly, and Shakespearean,

To my docs at PMH, especially Doctor Rob Buckman, who made me laugh through good times and bad and told me not to sell the furniture,

To the Toronto Arts Council, whose very generous grant gave me the time I needed to finish the book,

And to William Strachey, who, although he may not have been a source for Shakespeare, was certainly a source for me.

MORE GREAT FICTION FOR YOUNG PEOPLE

BAND OF ACADIANS
by John Skelton

978-1- 55488-040-9 / $12.99

In 1755, on the eve of the Seven Years' War, fifteen-year-old Nola and her Acadian parents face expulsion from Grand Pré by the British. Nola, her friends Hector and Jocelyne, Nola's grandfather, and a band of bold teenagers manage to flee by boat only to encounter challenges tougher than their wildest imaginings. Their destination is French-occupied Fort Louisbourg, but along the way hostile soldiers, a harsh environment, enigmatic Mi'kmaq, and superpowers at war turn their journey into a series of hair-raising adventures.

Will the resourceful teenagers finally discover what it takes to prevail in a continent poised on the edge of irrevocable change?

BILLY GREEN SAVES THE DAY
by Ben Guyatt

978-1- 55488-041-6 / $12.99

When the War of 1812 breaks out between the British in Canada and the United States, eighteen-year-old Billy Green is an expert woodsman with romantic ideas of combat. Struggling with his father's ideals and with his attraction to Sarah, the daughter of an American sympathizer, Billy soon finds himself faced with a series of fateful decisions.

Then, on June 5, 1813, he spots the massive American forces camped in the tiny hamlet of Stoney Creek. Against all odds, the young man rides three hours in the middle of the night to Burlington Heights to warn the British.

Can Billy Green help save the day? The ensuing historic battle will forever change the face of a nation and present Billy with challenges that will shake him to his very core.

BRIDGET'S BLACK '47
by Dorothy Perkyns

978-1- 55488-400-1 / $12.99

Bridget Quinlan is a spirited thirteen-year-old when the Irish potato famine of the 1840s shatters her life. Although her home is a hovel with few possessions, her family survives as long as her father can grow a good crop of potatoes on his small piece of land. Tragedy strikes when crops fail and typhus spreads, killing one of the boys in her school and then her brother, Rory.

With soldiers evicting the ill and unemployed, the Quinlans are forced to accept the offer of a passage to Canada. Appalling conditions onboard contribute to many deaths so that by the time they reach Grosse Île, Quebec, Bridget and her sister are alone in the world. The two are adopted by a kind farming family and gradually settle into their new life. After all the sadness and loss, a surprising turn of events brings them lasting joy.